STREET KILLER

Tom Philbin

FAWCETT GOLD MEDAL • NEW YORK

For Ken Pettus

A Fawcett Gold Medal Book
Published by Ballantine Books
Copyright © 1989 by Tom Philbin

All rights reserved under International and Pan-American Copyright Conventions. Published in the United States by Ballantine
Books, a division of Random House, Inc., New York, and si-
multaneously in Canada by Random House of Canada Limited,
Toronto.

Library of Congress Catalog Card Number: 89-91220

ISBN 0-449-14509-3

Manufactured in the United States of America

First Edition: September 1989

CHAPTER 1

The homicide scene was what jaded detectives of the Five
Three, more popularly known as Fort Siberia, called a
"grounder," because it looked like it would be easy to handle.

The dude reclining face up in the garbage-strewn foyer
of the fourth-floor, three-room rathole on 192nd and Creston had run a crack operation out of the apartment, and
though the door had been buttressed by carpenters so it
could withstand anything but direct mortar fire, that had
not protected the person ID'd as Charles "Chuckie" Perez.
When he pressed his dark, liquid eye against the door
peephole, somebody, instead of passing money through the
hole for crack, had inserted a PPK Walther and pulled the
trigger. It had, as one of the patrolmen called to the scene
commented, an "adverse effect on Chuckie's eye."

The thing was, nobody gave a shit about Chuckie. He
was part of the drug culture in the precinct. It could just as
well have been Chuckie on the other end of the PPK.

That's what happened when you dealt drugs: you died.

Crack had been almost entirely responsible for the increase in the mind-boggling number of homicides in the city, now close to two thousand for the year. The Five Three, after yielding its championship crown in homicide figures for one year to the Six Two in Brooklyn, now had vaulted back into its rightful spot. It was barely December and already there had been 101 killings in the precinct, two a week. Detectives in Siberia estimated that 90 percent of these homicides were related to drugs.

There were a number of people in the apartment in addition to the deceased.

Two beefy forensic technicians were working the scene for physical evidence, but essentially they were going through the motions, and knew it. This case would go into the drawer and turn yellow.

A police photographer was also on the scene. He would shoot fifteen or twenty color shots of the victim and surroundings. These, along with a number taken at the morgue, would also go into the official file.

One person who showed some concern was Vic Onairuts, a prematurely balding, intense, blue-eyed man who had come from the medical examiner's office to pronounce. Onairuts, who had been looking inside Chuckie's head for around two minutes, trying to determine what path the bullet took, was concerned not about Chuckie but about his own urge for a cigarette. For the last three years he had been off and on cigarettes a half a dozen times, and his latest assault on his habit had lasted for two weeks. But today, primarily because of a lot of pressure back at the office, he had felt a yearning to get that smoke tumbling among his bronchi again.

Only time would tell if he could resist.

The homicide scene was very ordinary-looking, except for one thing: the tall man standing directly behind Onairuts to whom the M.E. would occasionally speak.

He just didn't fit.

The man was over six feet tall, dark-haired, and handsome. He looked about forty.

He was dressed in a $1,000 light brown custom-made Canoli suit with an ultra-thin burnt orange stripe; a light gray Daniel Schagan shirt which cost $100; a muted, striped—gray, olive, brown—tie costing $50; slip-on, black, custom-made John Weston shoes costing $500. The outfit was accented by an olive pocket square handkerchief.

The only articles of clothing that indicated the man belonged at the scene were the clear vinyl gloves he wore.

The man was Detective First Grade George "The Bent One" Benton. He had been up for the next squeal at the Five Three Felony Squad.

Benton was disappointed with the homicide. He had investigated hundreds in his years at Siberia, and he knew better than anyone how ordinary this one was. Benton was disappointed because the case wasn't interesting enough to distract his attention from his own disappointing life.

Now, with Thanksgiving just past and Christmas not far away, Benton was thinking that he had not heard from his daughter, Beth, who had moved to Los Angeles with her mother. Benton's ex-wife, Joyce, had moved there with her dynamic new husband named Mel, who manufactured clothes hangers.

Benton wasn't surprised when Joyce didn't write or call or otherwise contact him. When they got divorced he more or less came to understand that she was totally into her own needs, and when she remarried he figured that was that. But Beth was another story.

Benton had a notebook out. Occasionally he would jot something down that Onairuts said as he examined the body.

Yes, Beth was another story. He had always been a good daddy to her, and she seemed to love him very much. The day she and Joyce left for California two years earlier she had cried and cried and told him she would write frequently. She said she didn't know how she could live without him.

In the beginning she did write. But as time had gone by he heard from her less and less. He had heard from her exactly once in the last three months. Benton knew Joyce tried to poison Beth against him, but he thought his love for Beth had made her impervious to Joyce's negative view of him.

But maybe not.

The situation was starting to make Benton feel like snakeshit, like he did just before he had the nervous breakdown in the squad room the day Joyce whacked him with divorce papers.

He didn't think it would come to another trip to the "Isle of Thorazine, hard by the county of Haldol." He was going to psychotherapy weekly, and he was much stronger than back in those dim days. Much stronger. Still, neglect tended to tear him down, put him on a track of self-criticism, where he battered himself about this, that, and the other thing.

His guilt could get bizarre. Once he had gone into a session with Dr. Stern and told him that he felt guilty about its being a rainy day. It was as if he had caused it, and he felt a need to go out in the street and apologize to passersby.

The corpse issued a short, angry fart and derailed his train of thought.

Well, there were some things to be thankful for, Benton thought. It was cold out—and in—and this combined with the fact that the body was fresh—a neighbor had called 911 to report a shot fired three hours earlier—kept the smell to a minimum. Plus the wind just broken was not what cops called a "death fart," which was of long duration and very potent.

Onairuts was finished. One of the patrolmen guarding the scene called the meat-wagon attendants, who were waiting downstairs to come up. Under Onairuts's direction, they secured the body in a carrier and hauled it out.

"When are you doing the post, Vic?" Benton asked.

Onairuts smiled at Benton. "Why do an autopsy? It's my opinion that this guy died from being shot in the melon."

Benton smiled slightly and nodded. Onairuts was quite obviously being driven mad by the lack of nicotine.

"How's nine tomorrow morning, George?" the M.E. asked.

"Fine. I'll be there."

"Have a nice day."

"Thanks."

Back at the Five Three, Benton immediately went up-stairs to the squad room, a bile-green room that featured a single filthy barred window that looked out on a battered brick wall, and an ambience that was always a blend of intestinal gas, alcohol, cigarette smoke, and coffee. Then again, to men who dealt with the aromas of a hundred homicide victims a year, the squad room could smell like a breath of fresh air.

He sat at one of the battered gray desks and used an ancient brown Royal typewriter to tap out a DD5 report on the demise of Charles "Chuckie" Perez.

Benton was a good writer; for a cop, he was superb. These days Bledsoe, the company commander, was so frustrated with report writing that he had actually delegated a couple of the cops to teach others English. Apparently the straw that broke Bledsoe's back was some patrolman writing that a priest was "cumming down Tremont Avenue" when he was assaulted.

Benton tapped the report out—he was a good typist, too—and then paused for a moment.

He felt a surge of yearning, but not without a surge of guilt.

Wouldn't it be great, he thought, to get a squeal like he had a year and a half ago?

They had discovered the body of a pretty young female nurse up on St. Bonaventure Street. She had been decapitated, and her vaginal vault had been excised.

Benton knew right away what it was: the work of a lustmurderer, a kind of serial killer.

The case had been a classic whodunit, and Benton had tracked a very dangerous perp on a five-state odyssey that had ended on a Bronx street not ten minutes from the station house, a confrontation in which Benton almost lost his life.

Albert Brooks. That was the killer's name.

Benton realized that a new lustmurderer was too rare to hope for. He just needed a case he could sink his teeth into, something to baffle and challenge him, something devious. Something that would make him forget that Beth didn't write.

But that wasn't the kind of case you usually got in Siberia. Here, killing was unsubtle. Quick action with a knife or a gun. Whodunits were very rare.

Still, you never knew for sure. He could hope, couldn't he?

CHAPTER 2

Fordham Road was a main thoroughfare that ran east and west across Fort Siberia and formed, in the minds of the cops who worked there, the dividing line between the regular bad Siberia and the truly *bad* Siberia. North of Fordham had no special name; south of Fordham, where craziness held sway, was nicknamed "Death Valley."

There were differences in both the physical condition and the activities of the inhabitants.

North of Fordham some buildings were abandoned and almost all needed repair. Halls were canvasses for the art of egoless Magic Marker artists, and many also served as bathrooms. If the house had heat—and most of these houses did have heat and hot water—the halls would be suffused with a stomach-churning smell that was a blend of ammonia and sulphur.

South of Fordham every other building was abandoned, and there were also two abandoned churches and a small hospital, all of which now served as shooting galleries.

North of Fordham there was plenty of crime, but not as

much as on the south side. In the current year, as of November 30, 82 of the 101 homicides had been committed south of Fordham.

At around 4:00 P.M., the same time George Benton was yearning for a whodunit he could sink his teeth into, Joseph "Little Joe" Rivera emerged from a three-story cream-colored brick building at the corner of the Concourse and Fordham Road. It was the main headquarters of the local Democratic Club.

Rivera started walking east along Fordham Road toward the municipal garage, where his car was parked.

Rivera was feeling good and looking good. He was dressed in a satin suit, and his silk shirt was open at the throat to reveal heavy gold chains and kinky little curls of chest hair on a solid, muscular light brown chest. His hair was glossy black; he wore a mustache, and his smile was brilliantly white. He was only five five, but he wore heels with lifts which added another four inches.

Little Joe felt particularly good because he figured very shortly he was going to be burying his *pinga* in the *zoftig* body of his nineteen-year-old secretary, Marcie Silverman, whom he had hired two weeks earlier.

Little Joe had hired her to be his secretary because she had two of the nicest tits he had ever seen; in the back of his mind as he interviewed her had developed the intention to show her how Puerto Ricans made love. Plus, of course, she typed well.

Today he had sensed that she was eyeing him. Little Joe was thirty-two. Young girls, he had learned, were intoxicated by older men who were rich and powerful.

Little Joe was powerful. He was a captain in the club, and he was rich.

In fact, as he walked along Fordham he was within walking distance of two buildings he owned under his sister's name. Both were in north Siberia. One was on 194th and Creston, and the other was across from St. James Park—nicknamed by residents "the pharmacy"—off Jerome Avenue.

Little Joe was also the secret owner of three other buildings in the Bronx, and in on a lot of other deals.

The buildings had a lot of welfare families in them; Little Joe had gotten to know the right people down at the Department of Human Services, so that clients were steered into his buildings, which were always full.

Rents were super-high, and not much maintenance was needed. He just tried to make sure that there was heat and hot water most of the time. Keep the beefing to a minimum.

As usual, Fordham Road was crowded. Christmas shopping had started in earnest, and windows and streets were festooned with decorations. There was a festive atmosphere that added to the good feeling inside Little Joe.

When he got to Creston, he considered taking a side trip the few blocks north to the house at 194th Street, then going across the park—it was still fairly safe when it was light out—to check on how things were going at the house off Jerome.

No one knew him at either of the houses—in fact at any of the houses he owned—and that was by design. If the tenants knew him by sight and he showed up, he might get into a bad beef. They considered him a slumlord. Maybe he was. But those animals who lived in the buildings would only ruin whatever he had fixed, so why keep doing it? If they thought he was so bad, they should try someone like that slimy hymie landlord in Brooklyn. His nickname was the Reptile.

Joe decided not to visit. It was close to darkness, anyway, and you didn't want to be walking the streets of this neighborhood after dark. Not unless you carried a gun.

A couple of times, as he neared the garage, people said, *Buenas tardes*. In his work as a captain of the club he got to know a lot of neighborhood people. He was always helping people out with jobs, problems with the Man, immigration, lots more. Helping translated into votes, which was the purpose of the club.

Little Joe enjoyed the popularity the job brought, and someday he hoped to be head of the club. If all went well down the line, he would be appointed a judge.

First, though, he and his amigos were going to have to get the hymies out of the top political jobs. They didn't belong. The Bronx was now 75 percent black and Hispanic. You shouldn't have Jews controlling things.

The municipal garage was a five-level, open-sided, poured-concrete structure located on Jerome and 191st Street. Little Joe always parked his black four-door XK-19 Jaguar in the garage because he knew it wouldn't last on the streets.

Willie, the black attendant, kept his eye on the car real good for him. Parked it near the booth where he could see it. Little Joe tipped him and the other guy, Ruben, good at Christmas.

Willie was on duty when Little Joe walked in the Jerome Avenue entrance—there was another on 191st.

"How you doin', my man," Rivera said to Willie, who was in the glassed-in kiosk near the front of the garage.

"Fine, Mr. Rivera," Willie said. "How you doin? How's the family?"

"Fine," Rivera said.

"Good. Been keeping a close eye on your black beauty." Willie expected that any day now the man would slip him at least a C note.

Rivera smiled. *"Bueno*, my man. *Gracias*."

Rivera went by the kiosk toward the car, which was maybe twenty yards away, parked with its front bumper against a wall. Willie could see it easily if he turned.

Willie had been reading—or perhaps gaping at would be more accurate—the latest issue of *Hustler*. He went back to it. He was particularly interested in a black fox spread over two pages; she had two of the nicest titties he had seen in a long, long time. And the nipples. They were fine too. Looked like little pancakes.

After a couple of minutes it occurred to Willie that Rivera's car had not been started.

He turned back and looked through the glass at the Jaguar.

Rivera was nowhere in sight.

Where the motherfuck had he gone?

Willie was about to get out of the booth to investigate when a car came in. The driver, a young white dude, took a ticket and drove in. At this hour, with all the shoppers' cars, he would have to go up to the fourth or fifth floor.

Willie turned toward Rivera's car again. There was still no one in it.

Willie went out of the kiosk and walked over to the passenger side of the car.

Rivera was still nowhere in sight.

Willie came around from the passenger side to the driver's side and froze.

"Motherfuck," he said out loud, feeling the blood drain from his face.

Rivera was lying faceup on the floor. There was some white foamy shit coming out of his mouth.

"Mr. Rivera?" Willie said. "Mr. Rivera?"

There was no answer. Willie started to run for the phone.

Chapter 3

As he dressed, Joe Lawless, Felony Squad commander at the Five Three, was surprised he was still happy. He had been very happy twenty minutes before, because tonight was to have been his first night off in months, and he and his fiancée, Barbara Babalino, had good seats for the Knicks-Celtics game. He had been looking forward to an evening cheering the Knicks on with Barbara, then having a couple of drinks and a late supper, and then home to bed and lovemaking till who knew when. Lawless wasn't on duty until four the next afternoon, and neither was Barbara, who was also a detective. Since tomorrow was Sunday, usually a slow day for felonies, he figured he would actually be able to stay out of the station house.

Then the phone had rung.

"Hey, Joe. It's Del Magee." Delano Magee was district attorney of Bronx County.

"Hey, Del, how you doin'?"

"Wonderful. About an hour ago we got a call from Jerry

12

Collins's attorney. Jerry wants to talk with me about cutting a deal."

"What kind of a deal?" Lawless asked.

"A reduction in sentence in return for bringing Toolan's world down around his ears."

"How come?"

"A few things. He says for one thing he didn't do the homicide he was convicted of. Also, he says that he feels Toolan set him up to take the fall, and third, that Toolan didn't help his wife while he was in Manhattan Correctional Center. Toolan's dealing millions of dollars a week, and his wife has to borrow money from her mother to pay the rent."

"He's facing twenty to life on the Kelly thing," Lawless said, referring to the homicide Collins had been convicted of in state court. "What would he want?"

"I don't know. His lawyer says he wants to get all interested parties together and talk. Then we'll see. But I don't want to talk unless you say okay. You've got too much time invested in putting Collins away. And no one needs to tell me how much you want Toolan. But I don't want to make any deal without you being part of it."

"I appreciate that."

"I think we should strike while the iron is hot," Magee said, "so I set up a meeting with Collins and his attorney for tonight at eight. What do you think?"

"Where?" Lawless asked.

"We're bringing him up to the fortress. Court 303. It'll be empty." By the fortress, Magee meant the Bronx County Courthouse.

"I'll be there."

"Good. See you."

Barbara was a cop, and she understood that the meeting at the fortress was more important even than a Knicks-Celtics game. In this case she was particularly understanding, since she also was assigned to the Five Three and had seen the results of Jimmy Toolan's handiwork.

"I'll go to the game," she said. "Maybe we can meet later."

"Fine," Lawless said. He was still happy. There would be other games and other nights off with Barbara. A chance like this to nail Jimmy Toolan might never come along again.

CHAPTER 4

Lawless drove to the Bronx County Courthouse in his battered white 1964 Impala. As he went along Pelham Parkway, he thought about Jimmy Toolan.

Toolan and his crew, the Bronxies, were roughly like the Westies, the group that terrorized the West Side of Manhattan for years. The crew was mostly Irish, people who had been raised in the Bronx, but there was also a sprinkling of Italians and other nationalities. Most of them were in their late thirties—Toolan was thirty-seven—and had known each other since they were kids.

In the Bronx, the Bronxies operated a good chunk of illegal activities—loansharking, drugs, extortion, murder, robbery, hijacking—and coexisted with the Jamaicans, Colombians, blacks, and others. And they were in close association with the Mafia. Lawless knew of at least four hits that Toolan and his crew had done for the Family.

Lawless had been going after Toolan and his crew for five years. The thing about them that made them so difficult to nail was their viciousness. Toolan had killed at least

15

twenty guys himself, and the crew had killed hundreds of people in their fight to control building projects, loan-sharking, and drugs. Anyone who dared to go against the Bronxies knew that Toolan or one of his crew would kill them as quick as look at them. In fact, Toolan seemed to enjoy killing. A police informant had put it best: "He'd rather kill somebody than get laid. Maybe to him it's the same thing."

Toolan's fearsome reputation as a street killer was enhanced by something he instituted when he got out of Attica four years earlier, after doing seven years for manslaughter. There he had learned how to butcher meat, and when he got out he started to butcher murder victims. In the crew, they called it the "Houdini act"—no corpus delicti, no prosecution.

People wondered: Did he do it because it was a good way to avoid detection—or because he enjoyed it?

Toolan had a long arm, a lot of friends in the right places. He had ways of finding and killing people. As long as you had money, there were people to corrupt. And since Toolan was funded by the Mafia, to which he paid a tithe of 10 percent, if you crossed Toolan, you crossed the Mafia.

Lawless, who was driving on Fordham, swung left on the Concourse and headed south.

Two years ago the police had fished a headless torso from the Bronx River and, through comparison of chest X rays—which revealed scar tissue from an old heart attack—were able to ID Sheldon "The Diamond" Finkel, a big-time mob loan shark who was closely affiliated with Toolan; he was Finkel's protégé and enforcer for at least five years. At one point, the Feds said, Finkel gave Toolan $150,000 in cash to buy a house in Jersey. But a year later Toolan lured Finkel into a bar on Webster Avenue off Fordham Road and he and three others in his crew shot Finkel and dismembered him. Word was that Finkel had entered the bar at ten and had left at eleven—in twelve pieces. The joke passed along Bronx streets was that the Diamond "came in in one at ten, and left at eleven in twelve."

The world of Toolan was, Lawless thought, a dangerous world to live in. Yesterday's buddy was today's dogmeat.

Lawless parked on the Grand Concourse—known simply to Bronxites as the Concourse—adjacent to Joyce Kilmer Park. One good thing about his car: it was so banged up that chances were reasonably good that it would be intact when he returned.

The fortress was aptly nicknamed. It was a huge white granite building featuring wide stone steps leading to massive entrance doors.

Lawless had spent a great deal of time in it. The Bronx was a war zone, and each year the court handled over nine thousand cases, the vast majority plea-bargained off the calendar. Sometimes it seemed to Lawless that eight thousand of the cases were generated in Siberia.

Inside, the structure was just as impressive as outside: the floors and walls were marble, the ceilings very high, all the doors wide and high.

As he walked across the lobby, Lawless realized he was a little nervous. And he knew why. He wanted very much to make a deal with Collins. Collins had to know as much about the Bronxies' operation as anyone. He had been Toolan's aide-de-camp for at least three years, ever since he got out of Otisville.

Collins was himself a stone killer—all the Bronxies were. But you had to look at the big picture. Toolan and the Bronxies were the cancer, and that's what he wanted to take out. He had to forget what a bad guy Collins was and concentrate on that. It was a rare opportunity, and he intended to take advantage of it.

CHAPTER 5

Dr. Victor J. Onairuts, with the help of a small, dark-haired, white-suited man known in the trade as a "deiner" (no one knew why the German word for helper was used) was making a canoe of Little Joe Rivera.

This particular removal of internal organs was, as they say, a priority job. Little Joe had been an important politician in the Fordham Road area, and Capt. Warren G. Bledsoe, CO of the Five Three, was getting pressure from the commissioner to clear it up quickly.

So present at the post was George Benton, whom Bledsoe didn't like—he thought he was crazy—but who he knew could get the job done when it came to an unusual death.

So far Onairuts had not discovered anything to indicate that the death was anything but natural.

Benton, despite his experience at homicide investigations and his attendance at hundreds of autopsies, didn't like it. He didn't mind the way the body was worked on, but he did worry about catching some fatal disease. Indeed,

18

he was always worried about that, and what better place to catch one than in the morgue, where fatal diseases were par for the course.

Onairuts lifted the glistening, dripping heart out of Little Joe's chest cavity. He cut into the arteries to see if he could see any deposits. *Nada.*

He placed the heart on a scale—basically the same kind of scale used in a butcher shop but stainless steel.

He intoned the weight into the tape recorder, and the deiner took the heart off the scale and placed it in a stainless steel pan.

Onairuts smiled at Benton. "That comes to $4.28. Will there be anything else today, Mr. Benton?"

Benton smiled slightly.

Within half an hour, everything was out in pans, and Onairuts looked at Benton. "I can't see anything, George," he said. "I don't know. It's puzzling. I can list it as heart failure, but this guy had very little plaque. In fact, without toxicological workups I'd say he's in excellent condition. I don't know why he died."

"When can you have the workups?"

"I don't know. I'll do a few standard tests and see what we get, okay?"

"Okay."

"But you can tell Bledsoe it's almost one hundred percent sure it's natural causes. It does happen."

"I will," Benton said.

An hour later, Benton exited the morgue.

He was annoyed. He tried to do a good job, but right now he was working twelve homicides, and he had to take valuable time away from them to investigate this.

He was annoyed, but he knew he wouldn't stand up to Bledsoe. Bledsoe was a mean guy mainly, and Benton figured he would just have to continue the investigation until he had enough paper in the file to satisfy the politicians.

CHAPTER 6

After leaving the morgue, which was located in downtown Manhattan, Benton took a subway uptown. There was no way you would catch him on a subway at night, but daytime was different. At this hour he figured that the predators who prowled the subways were all in their caves asleep.

He took the IND to 161st Street, then changed over to the IRT and took this to the Fordham Road stop. He walked one block north to the municipal garage.

The idea, as much as he loathed doing it, was to surprise witnesses. If a witness knew you were coming, you might get prepared answers. If you weren't expected, you got spontaneous answers. The latter were better.

Benton went into the garage. The black Jaguar that Rivera had owned was isolated with yellow crime scene tape.

Benton stopped at the kiosk. A thin black guy looked at him. "Are you Willie Brown?" Benton asked.

The thin guy nodded.

"I'm George Benton, with the Fifty-third Precinct. You

were on duty last night when Mr. Rivera came in to get his car, right?"

"Yeah," Willie said, "but I didn't see nothin'."

Benton waited while a car emerged from a ramp and stopped at the kiosk. He watched Willie ring up the ticket, take the money, and give change. The car drove away.

"Could you describe what happened?"

"Ain't nothin' happen. Mr. Rivera came in and went to his car. Didn't come out. Usually come out right away. When he didn't I went back there and found hisself lying on the ground with stuff coming out of his mouth—so I ran to call the poleece."

"How long was he back there?"

"Three, four minutes. Usually he come out within a minute."

"Did he make any noise? Cry? Yell?"

"I didn't hear nothin'."

"You didn't see him fall or anything?"

Willie shook his head.

"Thanks for your help."

Willie nodded, and he looked pleased. Benton got the feeling that he didn't like talking to cops.

Benton left Willie and walked over to the Jaguar.

For a moment he surveyed the scene, then ducked under the yellow tape and stood at the rear of the car. He looked down at the spot, outlined in chalk, where Rivera had lain.

The floor was gray concrete. There were black blotches and some powdery black stuff on the driver's side.

He checked the wall that the car was facing.

There was nothing there except an electrical outlet at baseboard level and, on the ceiling, an incandescent light in a cage.

Benton leaned down and looked into the interior of the Jag. The seats were gray velvet, the console rich mahogany. Everything was spotless.

There was, he thought, nothing here. The guy had died of some spontaneous coronary event—and that was that.

He knew he'd have to do a couple more interviews and get the toxicological results on the post from Vic Onairuts. He would also have to speak with Rivera's wife and talk with people he worked with at the Democratic Club before he could drop this in the drawer.

Rivera had lived in Riverdale, a section of the Bronx that was still nice, maybe because the rents were high and the people who usually created trouble couldn't afford them.

Or maybe it was because, like Arthur Avenue, some high-ranking Mafiosi lived in the area. If they didn't want you moving into the neighborhood, you didn't. If you tried, their solution was simple: they killed you.

The Riverdale area was much as it had been forty or fifty years earlier: street upon street of five- and six-story brick apartment buildings, still in good shape, every now and then interspersed with a cluster of private homes.

There were also some new condos. Rivera had lived in one of these, a large modernistic building that reminded Benton of a corncob on end.

Benton gave no notice that he was coming, though in this instance he felt lousy: he was going to be surprising a grieving widow. He would be asking questions to establish that she was not involved in the death of her husband nor had information that would lead to others who might be involved.

The doorman in the lobby called up on an intercom to announce that a detective wanted to see Mrs. Rivera.

"Send 'im up," the woman's voice replied.

On the eighth floor Benton rang the apartment bell and heard it chime melodiously inside.

The door opened and a heavyset woman, dressed in slacks and a shirt, looked up at him. She was wearing no makeup, and her hair was tied back.

"Mrs. Rivera?"

"Yes."

"My name is George Benton," he said, showing his tin. "I'm very sorry to disturb you at a time like this, but I'd like to have a few words with you about your husband."

She nodded and opened the door wide so Benton could enter. She closed the door behind him.

A short hall led to a massive living room that was expensively, though in Benton's opinion, garishly, decorated: heavy Mediterranean-style furniture, a light green wall-to-wall shag rug, bullfight paintings on the walls.

When she was in the middle of the room, Mrs. Rivera turned to him. "What do you want to know?"

Benton took out his notebook. "We have no reason to believe that foul play was involved in the death of your husband, but we have to check all bases. Do you know of anyone who might want harm to come to your husband?"

"Yeah," Mrs. Rivera said. "Me."

Benton blinked. "You?"

"Sure. I considered pinning that *maricón* to the mattress a number of times. But the sucker wasn't home long enough to let me get at him."

Benton smiled.

"Are you kidding?"

"You didn't know Little Joe. He was a bastard. But God—God knew what to do with him."

"Why was he a . . . what you said."

"Why? You got a week? I'll give you highlights. During our eleven illustrious years of marriage he probably laid a hundred different women; he was rarely home. He was a slumlord. He had an ego as big as this room. Plus he had a cruel mouth—he didn't give a shit about nobody but himself. I wasted a lot of years with him."

"Did he ever say anything about anyone having something against him?"

"I wouldn't know."

"Why not?"

"I haven't talked with him for almost two years, except to run the house."

Benton closed his notebook. "How was his physical condition? Did he ever complain about anything?"

Mrs. Rivera looked at Benton. "Can you come with me a minute?"

Benton followed her down a hall.

She stopped in front of a doorway down at the end of the hall. "This is what he did when he was home. Developed his body. But it didn't help, God knows."

Benton looked in. The room had been converted into a mini gym. Benton recognized some of the equipment because he too had worked out at one time, trying to perfect his body. Perhaps if he changed the exterior, the interior would improve too, he had hoped.

It didn't work. Changing the exterior was comparatively easy—the interior didn't budge.

Benton stepped inside and went over to a short refrigerator in the corner. He opened the door.

It was chock full of various health products. Benton recognized some of these, too.

He closed the refrigerator door and glanced around. Then he went out of the room and back to the living room. Mrs. Rivera followed.

"I don't think I have anything else," Benton said.

"When do you think your investigation will be finished?"

"A couple of days, no more."

"Good," Mrs. Rivera said, and for the first time since Benton had come into the apartment, she smiled.

"Insurance," she said, by way of explanation. "They won't release the money until the police investigation is over."

"Oh." And Benton thought: so much for the grieving widow.

CHAPTER 7

Barbara Babalino worked at the Five Three on what Captain Bledsoe called "female complaints"—all crimes against women, such as rape and wife beating. She also got involved when the perp was a woman, and in Siberia there was no dearth of women who committed crimes.

Barbara was in her small cubicle of an office on the main floor of the station house on the Monday after she had seen the Knicks and Celtics play when the desk lieutenant called back to her.

"There's a lady out here complaining about an annoying phone call. You want to come up?"

"Sure."

Barbara went to the front desk. A trim, pretty woman who Barbara estimated to be about fifty was standing there.

Barbara went up to her. "I'm Detective Babalino. Can I help you?"

"I hope so."

"What's your name?"

"Audrey Fontana."

"Why don't you come with me?"

The woman followed Barbara to her office.

"Please have a seat." Barbara gestured toward a chair in front of her gray metal desk. "Would you like some coffee?"

A glass coffee urn, half full, was on top of a hot plate set on a table in the corner of the office.

Mrs. Fontana sat down. "No thank you," she said.

Barbara smiled. "Smart lady."

Mrs. Fontana did not smile. She was nervous.

"How can I help you?" Barbara asked, as she sat down behind her desk.

"It's not much, maybe, but I just wanted to report an obscene telephone caller."

"When did this happen?"

"Friday. Friday afternoon about four o'clock."

"What happened?"

Mrs. Fontana explained that the caller said that his name was Dr. Sergeant and that he wanted to know if she knew where her daughter was. She didn't, and the caller said that he knew—that he had her daughter, Pat, who was eighteen, and that if she didn't do a certain something to herself, well, he didn't say, but he implied something bad would happen.

Mrs. Fontana's eyes misted.

Barbara got up and went around the desk. She put her hand on Mrs. Fontana's shoulder. "Want some water or something?"

"No, I'm okay. It's just that I don't know what I'll do if he calls back."

Barbara sat back down at her desk. "I don't think he will, but there are ways to protect yourself—there are about 200,000 of these calls statewide every year."

"What should I do?"

"You have some options. If you want, you can screen your calls with an answering machine."

"I don't have one of those."

"Okay," Barbara said. "If he or anyone else calls, just hang up. Don't say anything—don't get involved in any conversation with him. And don't tell anyone about the calls."

"Why?"

"Sometimes it's friends of friends who are calling, and your getting upset would be an incentive for them to call again."

"What sick people!"

"They are sick," Barbara agreed. "Do you want to make out a formal complaint?"

"Yes."

"Good."

Barbara typed up a complaint form, Mrs. Fontana signed it, and then Barbara walked her out of the station house, reassuring her again.

A few minutes after Mrs. Fontana left, Barbara was standing outside the glassed-in square that housed that cop's cop, Captain Warren G. Bledsoe, who was on the phone. She felt the eyes of Fletcher, his oily aide, who sat at a desk outside the office, working her over.

Barbara said nothing. She watched Bledsoe. She figured that among the horde of misfits who had been shipped to Siberia, there were a lot of good cops. Bledsoe wasn't one of them. He had been shipped there because of a lost power play at One Police Plaza. It was headquarters' gain and Siberia's loss.

Bledsoe hung up and saw Barbara. He crooked his finger for her to come in.

Barbara was pissed at this Dr. Sergeant. There was something she had not told Mrs. Fontana: it was not the first time they had received complaints about Dr. Sergeant. In fact, he was a legend in the tri-state area. Over the last twenty years he had made thousands—maybe ten thousand—obscene calls.

None of this, Barbara knew, mattered to Bledsoe. What mattered to him was one thing: his self-interest. And everything had to be presented to him in light of this.

"We've got another complaint on Dr. Sergeant."

Bledsoe had very heavy eyebrows and a bald dome. He resembled the actor Edward Asner. He used his eyebrows for theatrical effect. "So?"

"I think it's about time I went after this guy in a major way. He's caused a lot of pain."

Bledsoe raised his eyebrows. His ample nose twitched as if he had smelled something foul. "Babalino, who has he harmed?"

"No one, but he's disturbed a lot of people. And he's been allowed to break the law for twenty years."

"You've got too much on your plate to go after this guy."

"Captain, I'm not talking about going after him full time. Just more than we are now, which is nothing."

"I can't allow it. You've got your priorities."

Barbara thought about asking whether people should have to live in fear that the next time they pick up the phone an obscene jerk is going to be on the other end.

But she didn't. She knew it would fall on the ears of a jerk, and for the moment, at least, she didn't know how to convince Bledsoe of anything. She left the office, feeling Fletcher's eyes on her as she walked away.

CHAPTER 8

Delano Magee and Joe Lawless were sitting in a booth in the back of a luncheonette in the shadow of the el and Yankee Stadium on 161st Street. Every now and then the el would rumble by. It was night of the second day they had been interrogating Jerry Collins. Magee had called an end to it.

Lawless and Magee were both working on black coffee, the official drink of law enforcement personnel.

"So how would you evaluate what he gave us?" Lawless asked.

"Good stuff. He's obviously telling the truth. You heard what I told him. If I catch him in a lie, he's gone for good."

Lawless, who was smoking a cigarette, nodded. "So you got enough to indict Toolan?"

"Definitely. The question is, can we convict?"

Lawless looked at Magee. Something was bothering the district attorney. "What's the matter, Del?"

"I'm a little concerned about this whole deal. You know

the Manhattan DA has tried Toolan twice, and twice he's gotten off. Now the DA didn't have anyone as close to Toolan as Collins, but I'm worried that if we don't have an airtight case he'll walk. We're going to have to pick one crime, try him on that, and hope we win."

"I sense you've got something up your sleeve."

Magee nodded. "Can't fool you, can I, Joe? I do. But have you ever heard the saying 'Sic transit gloria mundi'?"

"It's Latin, right?"

"Means 'Thus pass the glories of the world.' Well, that would be the case here. We'd have to give primary responsibility to the Feds—because with their laws, and Collins as a witness, they could definitely get Toolan, and maybe others as well."

"RICO?" Lawless asked, referring to the Racketeer Influenced Corrupt Organization law, which was originally designed to fight organized crime but had been used widely and successfully in other prosecutions.

"Absolutely. You know, Joe, the burden of proof is not as great as in a state trial. And they would prosecute Toolan and the whole gang as a criminal enterprise. What I can think of right now, based on Collins's statement, is murder, attempted murder, extortionate use of credit, conspiracy to sell drugs, selling drugs, extortion . . . the list goes on and on. All the Feds would have to prove is two of those charges against each gang member to establish a pattern of racketeering, and they'd be guilty under RICO. That carries twenty years for the RICO count and twenty for each of the counts they're guilty of. I think once they were charged under RICO, gang members would start to flip."

"Sounds good."

"But you and I might well be minor players in this thing. I'm sure they'll use us, but . . ."

"I'll tell you, Del, I don't think I'm ready to give up anything on nailing Toolan. I've tried to nail him for five years—and I've got seven guys on a squad who've done

30

the same thing. If we give this to the Feds and they start to shut us out . . . bad news."

Magee nodded. "Even if it meant Toolan walking?"

Lawless ground his cigarette butt out in an ashtray on the table. Feeling guilty, because Barbara was always nagging him about his smoking, he lit another.

"No. I wouldn't want to run this case if it meant Toolan walked. I wouldn't allow that. But I don't think it's an either-or situation. I think my squad can and should run the investigation—and also be responsible for the safety of Collins. We've dealt firsthand with Toolan. I would never underestimate him."

"I agree with you," Magee said. "Why don't we talk to them and see if they're interested—which I think they definitely will be—and what would be what?"

"Fair enough."

At three in the afternoon of the next day, Lawless and Magee sat in the office of Mary Lee Baxter, an assistant U.S. attorney for the Southern District of New York.

Over the last couple of years, Mary Lee had handled most of the high-profile cases the Feds had gotten involved in in the district. She had a reputation among cops as a tough and good prosecutor. On one wall there were B shots—standard front and side views—of various criminals who knew just how good she was. They were all serving big time in various federal prisons throughout the country.

Mary Lee Baxter was the classic case of the container giving no indication of what the contents were. She was in her late thirties, a slim, pretty woman with prematurely gray hair who didn't have to wear a lot of makeup to look seductive.

They exchanged small talk. Magee was a former prosecutor with the Southern District, though he had not known Mary Lee. She knew of him and knew Lawless—he had worked with the Feds on a number of joint NYPD-Fed operations.

A few minutes after they arrived they got down to business.

Magee laid it all out. Mary Lee was very familiar with Toolan and the Bronxies, having heard frequently about their savagery over the last ten years.

She looked at Magee in silence for a moment after he had finished speaking. "I like it," she said. "It sounds like you've got a lot. But what does Collins want?"

"His lawyer first said he wanted him to walk, but we explained that there was no way that would be possible. We were hovering around five to fifteen."

"I would have to clear that with the Bossman, but it sounds okay to me."

"Also," Magee said, "we would like to retain investigatory supervision of the case, since Joe and his team have worked on the Bronxies so long."

Mary Lee smiled. "I'd be a fool to want someone else. I wouldn't bring in a new chef just before the biggest party of the year."

They all laughed.

"Of course," she added, "we would want to have some of our own people on it. But the investigations could be parallel. Our top guy could keep in touch with Joe to make sure the left hand knows what the right hand is doing."

"Who would have overall responsibility?" Lawless asked.

"You," she said.

Lawless nodded.

"One other thing," Magee said. "Once Toolan finds out about this he'll put a contract out on Collins, and probably his family. We want to supervise his protection."

"Toolan might have a contract out on him already," Lawless said. "Collins got twenty to life on the state conviction. Toolan might be thinking that anyone facing that amount of time might become a pigeon."

"What would you do with him?" Mary Lee asked.

"Nobody would know," Lawless said. "Just me and the people guarding him."

"Take him out of prison?"

"Probably," Lawless said. "Even in protective custody he could be vulnerable."

"As I said, it sounds as if you have a strong case here, but we could buttress it if we could get Toolan on a wire. I was thinking," Mary Lee said, "if Toolan doesn't know that Collins has flipped, maybe we could get his wife to wear a wire and meet with him and—"

Lawless interrupted. "That would be very dangerous. Toolan has a thing about wires. He's been known to be in a restaurant, out eating, and suddenly he commands everyone with him—men and women—into the men's room to strip. We might be feeding her to the dogs."

"Maybe someone else, then," Mary Lee said. "I just want to get another witness to corroborate what Collins said. That way it would be easier to create a domino situation—everybody's flipping to save themselves."

"Right," Magee said. It was precisely the point he had made to Lawless.

"We'd have to make sure that Toolan wasn't around when Francie was with whoever," Lawless said. "He would suspect her."

"What about Collins himself wearing a wire?" Mary Lee suggested. "If we could find some other target close to Toolan."

"I think all the Bronxies would be leery of Jerry," Lawless said. "Francie has a much better chance of not setting off alarm bells."

"Of course we don't know if Francie would cooperate," Magee said.

"The government would be willing to pay," Mary Lee said. "I think I could get Rudy to spring for twenty thousand on this. So what they'd be getting is a nice package —reduced sentence, witness protection program, and

$20,000. When Collins gets out he has a shot at taking up his life."

Magee turned to Lawless. "Any candidates for her to talk to?"

"She knows all Toolan's intimates," Lawless said. "Maybe she could suggest someone."

"Good," Mary Lee said. "We also could use some corroborating physical evidence."

"That's not going to be that easy," Lawless said. "You know, Toolan does his Houdini act with bodies."

"Right," Mary Lee said.

"Who's going to approach Francie Collins?" Magee asked.

"Let's talk to Collins," Lawless said, "and have him talk to her. I think that's safest at this point."

The prosecutors nodded.

Mary Lee stood up. From a large red tin she took a pretzel. "Anybody care for a pretzel?"

Lawless and Magee declined.

Mary Lee bit into the pretzel. "Let's sum it up," she said, walking to the window that looked out over a complex of buildings that included St. Andrew's Church and police headquarters. "We're going to have two teams of detectives under the ultimate supervision of Joe Lawless, but the teams will operate more or less independently. If there is a conflict, incidentally, I would like to be informed."

"No problem," Lawless said.

"Someone's going to approach Collins and ask him to ask his wife to wear a wire—for $20,000. No one must know about it, not even his lawyer. Right?"

"Absolutely," Magee said.

"We start protecting Collins now. You guys are responsible for that."

"Right," Lawless said.

"Also," Mary Lee added, "the detective teams will be looking for corroborating physical evidence."

34

"Right," Lawless said.

Mary Lee had consumed the pretzel. She looked at the tin again, then forced herself to look away.

The meeting was almost over. Lawless and Magee stood up.

Mary Lee looked up at them. "I want to thank you guys for coming to me. Del, I think we have a much better chance to bring the Bronxies down with RICO than you would have had, but a lot of prosecutors wouldn't have given the case up."

"I grew up on the streets of the Bronx," Magee said. "I had some dreams that came true—I'm parked in a posh office in the fortress. But I had some friends who had some dreams too, and they're in the cemetery because of drugs and guys like Jimmy Toolan. The day I forget that is the day it stops having any meaning for me."

Lawless looked at him. Not all of the glories of the world, he thought, had passed.

CHAPTER 9

The night they talked to Mary Lee Baxter, Lawless and Magee arranged a special visit for Francie Collins to see her husband in one of the empty courtrooms on the third floor of the fortress. Only Lawless, Magee, and the Collinses were there.

Magee laid it out for them.

When he was finished, Jerry Collins was quiet, but Magee and Lawless both sensed that he liked the idea.

"What do you think, Jerry? Francie?" Magee asked.

Jerry Collins, who, like almost all the Bronxies, was short, was leaning against one of the tables. He had a troubled look on his very Irish face. "The only thing I don't like about it," he said, "is the money. That's not much to pay Francie for risking her life."

Magee, who was sitting down, got up. "Let's go, Joe," he said. "Let's go, Jerry."

"What'sa matter?" Jerry asked.

"You're trying to work us," Magee said. "You should

know better than that. That's the deal. It's a package. Take it or leave it."

"All right," Jerry said. "I'll take it."

His wife nodded.

Everybody got resettled.

"Okay, now we have the question of *who*. Who can Francie talk with?" Magee said.

"Charlie," the Collinses said in unison. "Charlie McCoy."

"Yeah," Jerry continued. "He's always shooting his mouth off about something because he's pissed that Jimmy demoted him."

Lawless knew the story. Charlie McCoy had long been a high-ranking Bronxie, but Toolan demoted him when he started to use too much of the product he sold—pills.

"He's lucky he didn't get fucking clipped," Jerry said. "But it may yet fucking happen. Jimmy don't like no one with loose lips. And if he figures you got a loose lip and can hurt him, he'll whack you sure as the sun comes up in the morning."

"How many times have you talked with him, Francie?" Lawless asked.

"A few times. I usually avoided him."

"Yeah, he's always had the hots for my old lady." Jerry looked at Francie. She was a small woman with disproportionately large breasts. She was dark-haired, and pretty in a hard way. "He'd be good," Jerry added. "His cock would be up and his guard down."

They all laughed.

"Can you make contact with him so it's not obvious?" Magee asked.

Jerry thought a moment, then said. "He hangs out at the Five Ninety-two Club. Always trying to pick up broads. Play the big man. Maybe Francie could go in there."

"Is there a quiet place there?" Lawless asked.

"It's quiet between sets," Jerry said.

"Yeah. No point wearing a wire if nothing can be heard."

"How many times you think I'll have to see him?" Francie asked.

"Once should be enough, if we're lucky," Lawless said.

"What am I going to say when I see him?"

There was silence.

"Have you ever been in the club?" Lawless asked.

"Sure. When me and Jerry was courtin'."

"Okay," Lawless said. "Just go in and sit at the bar. When Charlie approaches you and asks you why you're there, just tell him it's because you miss Jerry so much. You feel better in a place where you used to have such a good time."

"I like that," Francie said.

"And then just take it from there."

"Yeah," Jerry said. "When he tries to get into your pants." He laughed.

"Good," Magee said.

Jerry was looking at Francie in a strange way. "I was wondering," he said, "if I could have a little time alone with Francie now?"

"You're going to be in a safe house together soon," Magee said.

Jerry looked at him. Words were unnecessary. Magee and Lawless thought about it. The room had only one exit; the windows were barred.

"Okay, Joe?" Magee asked.

Lawless nodded.

"Okay," Magee said. "Leave the place the way you found it."

Ten minutes later, Jerry and Francie came out of the courtroom.

"Okay?" Magee asked.

"More than okay," Jerry said.

CHAPTER 10

Her name was Ginger, and she was twenty years old. Now, as she looked into the full-length mirror of the apartment she shared with her mother on Mosholu Parkway and Webster Avenue, she saw again just how foxy she was.

She was standing sideways, her long wavy blond hair down almost to the midpoint of her back, her face at a three-quarters angle to the glass.

She had on a leather jacket with the colors of the MC group she belonged to, and denim pants. Her jugs jutted out, and so did her backside, but not too much. She watched her weight. The difference between a great ass and a fat ass was five pounds.

Completing her outfit were scuffed black leather boots. Various keys and chains hung from her jacket and pants.

She rolled back her sleeves so the tattoos could be seen on her forearms. One said DAVE, and the other was the wings emblem of Harley-Davidson motorcycles. She had two other tattoos—a beautiful butterfly on the top of her left boob, and a snake that wrapped around her right thigh, with its head pointing toward her pussy.

She turned and stepped close to the mirror. Her makeup looked good. Heavy lipstick, heavy mascara. Foxy lady!

The phone, which was on a small table near the bed, rang.

She picked up after the second ring. "Yeah?" she said.

"My name is Dr. Sergeant. Is this Joan?"

"Yes it is," Ginger said. Ginger's mother, Joan, was a waitress downtown and had lots of boyfriends. Sometimes Ginger liked to fuck around with them.

The man said, "Do you know where your daughter, Ginger, is?"

Ginger smiled. This was funny. "No. Where?"

"She's with me. And unless you do something for me you're not going to see her again."

"What's that?" Ginger said, her voice flat.

"First, let me ask you: What color underwear are you wearing?"

"Red with brown skid marks, you perverted mother-fucker! This is Ginger. Stick it up your chocolate speed-way!"

And Ginger slammed the phone down.

Dr. Sergeant was pissed, and his thing had gone down to half-mast. He had to make another call.

Mrs. Helen Archer had three locks on the door: the regular lock, the dead bolt, and the Fox security lock, the kind where one end of a bar leans against the door and the other end fits into a metal cup sunk into the floor.

But, though she lived on 198th and Creston, not in Death Valley, she still didn't feel secure. Mrs. Archer knew she was fair game.

So Mrs. Archer spent a lot of time at her window, which faced Walton Park, dreaming about yesterday, when she and Ray, her husband, and their two kids had been happy

40

in the apartment. Back then, years ago, the park was clean and well-maintained, and the kids could play there in safety until all hours of the night.

But that was gone—most of the grass had been worn off, replaced by vast brown bald areas—and Ray was gone, and her two daughters, both of whom lived on the West Coast.

Her daughters had urged her to leave the neighborhood, but she had not done so yet. She didn't know why. She knew she just hated the idea of change, all the uprooting that would be involved. In fact, she had been born only two blocks from where she now lived, and had gone to all the local schools.

She hated locking herself up. Not just because it made her feel like she was living in a fort, but also in a practical sense: if a fire ever broke out she might have a hard time getting out safely.

Or she might have a heart attack. She suffered angina attacks, and the doctor had told her to take it easy, avoid exertion and stress. Easy for him to talk. He lived in a big safe house on Long Island.

Now she was sitting by the window, looking out at kids playing with dogs in the center grass. It seemed everybody owned either a police dog or a Doberman pinscher or one of those terrible pit dogs. Whatever happened, she wondered, to ordinary dogs, like cocker spaniels and golden retrievers? If the dog wasn't capable of hurting someone, the people around here wouldn't own it.

The phone rang, a welcome sound to Mrs. Archer. Most of her day was spent watching TV, listening to the radio, or trying to read. When someone called, anyone—a few months ago she had happily answered a phone survey—it broke up her day and made her feel less lonely.

She picked up: "Hello?"

"Helen Archer?"

"Yes."

"This is Dr. Sergeant."

"Are you affiliated with Dr. Miller?" Dr. Miller was the internist she went to.

"No, I'm not, Helen."

"Oh. How can I help you?"

"Do you know where your daughter is?"

"What?" Mrs. Archer said, with a trace of concern. "My daughter?"

"Your daughter Mary."

"Who is this?"

He spoke low and fast and gutturally, and Mrs. Archer felt her pulse rate elevate.

"This is Dr. Sergeant, bitch. I've got Mary. Answer my questions if you want her back."

"Please . . ."

"What color is your underwear?"

"Please don't hurt Mary."

"What color is—"

"White."

"Pull up your dress and stick your arthritic hand through the old pubic hair and then stick your finger into your pussy and manipulate it."

"Oh, please. Oh . . ."

Mrs. Archer felt a little faint, then sweaty. God. She felt pain in the center of her chest. She couldn't think. The pain was growing . . . and then she felt pain suddenly gripping her left arm. Oh God, she thought, I'm having a heart attack. I'm . . .

She hung up. Her vision was getting cloudy. She could feel her heart racing. She tried to think. Get to the door. Get to the door.

No. Call.

She dialed 911.

"My name is Archer. I live at 2456 Creston, number 3A. Please send someone. I'm having a heart attack."

"We're on our way."

Please hurry, she thought.

The door. She had to make it to the door.

42

She staggered. She felt as though she was made of Jell-O. The pain in her chest was getting bigger, as if there was a hand inside her chest and it was squeezing her. She was sweating, she felt very faint. . . .

She got the Fox lock off. Will someone break in? she thought.

She started to unfasten the dead bolt. Then, suddenly, the world in front of her eyes was no more, and she fell to the floor.

CHAPTER 11

Since the Chuckie Perez squeal had come in, two more cases had come Benton's way. One was a murder, the other an autoerotic death.

The murder was of a pregnant prostitute with AIDS. Rumor in the street said that she was killed in retaliation against her common-law husband, a drug dealer who had provided information to police on other dealers.

Benton figured they would make an arrest on that shortly.

The autoerotic case was interesting. A guard in a warehouse had lain down on a bunch of blankets, the bottom one of which had double-faced carpet tape on it. Then he had encased his genitals in a Baggy and rolled himself up like a sealed cigar. Problem was, he couldn't get out, and he had asphyxiated.

Onairuts had gotten back the toxicological results on Rivera and they were negative.

Benton had no way to go. Everything started and ended in the M.E.'s office. The M.E. said that Rivera had died of something, unexplained, that caused cardiac arrest.

That should have been it. But this was political, so Benton had to take the investigation a little further. He had learned that Rivera's assistant at the Democratic Club was someone named Marcie Silverman. Benton would talk with her—and that would be it.

The club opened at five, and Benton arrived shortly thereafter.

He climbed one long flight of stairs, which let out into a large room that reminded him of an unemployment agency. There were lines of desks in the center and tiny offices around the perimeter.

Most of the desks were empty, but he went over to a young Hispanic guy who was on the phone. The guy hung up just as Benton arrived at the desk.

"Excuse me," Benton said. "Could you tell me where Marcie Silverman is?"

"Yeah. She's over there, in the green dress."

The man pointed to a young, pretty woman sitting at a desk in one corner of the room.

Benton went over to her.

She looked up.

"Are you Marcie?"

"Yes."

"My name is George Benton. I'm a detective from the Fifty-third Precinct, and I'm looking into the death of Mr. Rivera. Do you have time for a few questions—strictly routine."

A wave of sadness passed across her face, then it was gone. She nodded. "Please have a seat."

Benton sat down in a straight-back chair next to the desk and took out his notebook.

"Isn't it terrible what happened?" she said. "He was only thirty-two. It's hard to believe."

Benton nodded. "Yes, it is shocking."

There was a pause.

"What I'm trying to do," he said, "is determine exactly

45

how Mr. Rivera died—mainly that no foul play was involved."

"I see."

"Do you know if Mr. Rivera was on any special medication?"

"No."

"He wasn't under the care of a doctor?"

"Not that I know of."

"I see." Benton paused. He sensed that this girl was feeling this guy's death bad. He had to be careful.

"Let me ask you this. And I have to. I'm sorry. Do you know if Mr. Rivera was on any drugs like cocaine?"

She shook her vigorously. "No way. To Joe—Mr. Rivera—his body was a temple. He would never put garbage like that in it."

"I see," Benton said.

He paused again.

"If someone were to ask you how Mr. Rivera died, what would you say?"

"I'd say I have no idea. It's unexplainable."

"I see." Benton looked down at his notebook. Some of the girl's perfume drifted into his nostrils.

He looked up.

"That's about it." He smiled. "Except I have to ask you the one question they always ask on TV. Do you know of anyone who would want to harm Mr. Rivera?"

"I did hear of one person."

Benton blinked.

"Who was that?"

"Joe—Mr. Rivera told me about it. He said he was in a restaurant . . ."

"When was this?"

"About a month ago . . . having dinner with some friends, and some nut came up to the table and told them that they all owed reparation or something. That if they didn't do something he was going to kill them. Mr. Rivera laughed about it."

46

"What did the person who said this look like?"

"Mr. Rivera didn't say. I do remember he called him a 'witch doctor.' And he did say he called him."

"When?"

"Just a few days ago."

"Did he say what he said?"

"No."

"At this dinner," Benton said, "did Mr. Rivera say who was with him?"

"I do know that Herb Kellner was there and . . . I think Dave Gold. I'm not sure who else."

"Do you have Mr. Kellner or Mr. Gold's number?"

"Oh, sure."

Marcie Silverman flipped through a Rol-a-dex on her desk, wrote each of the names and numbers on a slip of paper, and handed it to Benton. He glanced at it to make sure he could read it, then slipped it into his notebook.

He stood up.

"Thank you so much for your help. There's not much anybody can do in a situation like this. Time is the only thing that helps."

"Thank you, Mr. Benton."

Benton left. Witch doctor? he thought. This case wasn't quite ready to put in a drawer.

CHAPTER 12

It was five thirty when Benton called the two numbers Marcie Silverman had given him.

Both were Manhattan numbers. When he called the Kellner number, he got a secretary who said that Mr. Kellner had gone for the day. She said that Benton, who did not say who he was, could call back in the morning. Benton jotted down the name of Kellner's company—HK Associates.

The Gold number was answered by a secretary as Wishbone Properties. Benton identified himself when he found Gold was in. Gold got on the phone. Benton said only that he wanted to speak to Gold about Joseph Rivera's passing.

"I heard about it," Gold said. "But they said he just dropped dead."

"I'll talk to you about it when I see you," Benton said. "When could that be?"

"Come on over now."

* * *

The building that housed Wishbone Properties was on 53rd Street off Madison Avenue. It was like the other buildings on the street—an immense glass box. Now, in the evening, it reflected the lights of the city.

As he entered, Benton remembered how going downtown intimidated him when he was a kid. Everything was so big and unfriendly. It still was, but he was less intimidated.

The building was officially closed, so the security guard had to have Benton sign in and call up.

Wishbone Properties was located directly opposite the elevator on the nineteenth floor.

The name was hand-painted in a beautiful calligraphic script on an all-glass wall. The reception area was a carnival of colors—mauve walls, tan desk, apple-green wall-to-wall rug. It struck Benton, who used to do some house painting when he was young, that if you mixed the colors together and added a dash of red you would get beige.

The receptionist was dressed in white, as if the decorator thought that one more color would be excessive and had told her to dress in a neutral color.

She was a pretty woman of about thirty with glossy upswept black hair and fairly dramatic makeup. She had a nice body.

"May I help you, sir?"

"Yes. I'm George Benton, with the NYPD. Mr. Gold expects me."

"Just a moment, please," she said. Just a little warmth had gone out of her smile.

She punched the intercom.

"Detective Benton is here."

She listened, then hung up.

"Can you come with me, please?"

Benton followed the young woman down a long, carpeted hallway to a corner office that featured an acre of carpet and a spectacular view of the city through floor-to-ceiling windows.

Gold came out from behind his desk. Benton fixed him at about fifty. He was overweight, and his shirt opened at the throat to reveal curls of chest hair. He was wearing a blondish toupee, and his teeth looked capped; there was a pinky ring on each hand.

Benton's instant reaction was dislike. Gold reminded him of Mel, the guy Joyce had married. Brash, confident, sexual tiger.

Benton pushed the thought away. He was a cop, and his personal stuff had no place in this room.

Gold shook Benton's hand and offered him a seat.

Benton sat down.

Gold sat back down behind his desk. "How can I help you, sir?" He oozed oil.

"We've been told that a few weeks ago you were at a restaurant with Mr. Rivera and some other people and were accosted by someone who threatened you."

"Oh, that," Gold said. "You think that's related to Rivera's death?"

"I don't know," Benton said. "What happened?"

"We were in this restaurant, Amalfi's, downtown, and while we were there this guy comes in. He was a black guy dressed in a black suit and a black T-shirt. He had very weird light blue eyes—I mean you know colored guys have dark eyes, right?—and he just stands at the table and says to us real quietly that we are slumlords and that we must give up Parcel 19 or die. 'You stole the land from the people,' he said, 'and they want it back. If you don't give it back I will make you die.' And then he placed a bloody chicken heart on the table—some kind of voodoo thing, I guess."

"What's Parcel 19?"

"Nothing," Gold said. "It's a hunk of land we own in the South Bronx."

"Who's 'we'?"

"Me, Herb Kellner, Rivera, and Frank DeVito. We own separate companies, but a few years ago we bought a par-

50

cel of land in the South Bronx as a speculation, if the Bronx comes back someday. So far that hasn't happened. I don't know why anyone would want us to give that parcel back to the city."

"That's who would get it back if you gave it up?"

"Yes."

"What happened after the man said that?"

"He just left. It took no more than thirty seconds and he was gone. I mean he took a chance doing it at Amalfi's, too, because I think Leo Amalfi knows some pretty rough people."

His voice trailed off.

"Did he call you a few days ago?"

"The black guy?"

Benton nodded.

"Yeah. A few days ago. He called himself 'the demon of the people,' I think, and said I was in danger because I hadn't followed instructions and given up Parcel 19."

"Did he call your partners?"

"I don't know."

"What do you think of all this?"

"I don't think anything. Rivera died on his own. I don't think it has anything to do with a witch doctor. That's bullshit. Rivera's death was just a coincidence."

"What did the others think?"

"I don't know."

"Did Rivera ever mention anything else unusual?"

"Not really. Anyway, my contact with him is limited. We have this partnership on Parcel 19, and that's about it."

"I see," Benton said. "And you're not planning to acquiesce to this witch doctor's demands?"

"No way."

Benton stood up. "Mr. Gold, thanks for your help."

Benton took a business card out of his jacket pocket. It had his name and the number of the squad room on it. "If you think of anything else, please give me a ring."

"Sure will."

Benton found his own way out of the office. The front desk was unoccupied.

As he rode down, he thought that Gold was quite forth-coming, unlike his image. He looked and talked oily, yet he spoke honestly. Of course, Benton thought, that too could be part of the oiliness.

CHAPTER 13

From Gold's, Benton went back to the squad room.

A couple of detectives—Loomis and Regan—were at desks on the phone, but otherwise the squad room was empty. In his fourteen-year career as a cop Benton had been in five different station houses, and, since he had made detective nine years earlier, he had worked out of four different squad rooms. The one at Siberia was much more frequently empty than the others—the cops were usually out on the street confronting new business. Many did their paperwork at home.

He checked the "squeal book," in which Lawless required squad detectives to list the crimes that came in. Lawless liked everyone in the squad to know what everyone else was doing. Sometimes there was case overlap, and detectives could provide helpful information for each other. And you could see at a glance if there was a pattern of crimes occurring.

There was only one thing in the book, a suicide, and it saddened Benton. He certainly had never been able to steel himself completely—though other cops seemed to have—against the mayhem of crime. Suicides were particularly upsetting, though he never showed outwardly that they bothered him. It was just something cops didn't do—they held stuff in.

But he understood the psychodynamics of suicide.

When he had been going through his divorce, he had considered "eating his thirty-eight," and while he was at South Oaks Psychiatric Hospital two of the patients had killed themselves, an old lady and a young guy. The old lady had just walked into a lake on the property, and the guy had hung himself.

There would be more suicides now. Christmas was the most popular time for killing yourself, followed by spring. Benton thought of the lines from T. S. Eliot: "April is the cruelest month . . . mixing memory with desire . . ."

The listing said: *Male, hispanic, Jose Morales, 35, apparent suicide (hanging), 238 West Tremont, 1830 hours, this date.*

Benton got himself a cup of coffee. Once, when someone had been joking about his hypochondria, he said that's why he drank the squad room coffee: no germs or cancer cells could live in the same system with that coffee.

He sipped the coffee—yes, this stuff would kill every invader inside his body—and looked through the filthy barred window at the brick wall. Or, more precisely, he looked at the wall through his reflection.

What was a young Hispanic doing killing himself? he wondered.

Benton guessed he understood. Something, somewhere had gotten to be too much for him, and he had ended it.

Benton knew some members of the squad referred to Hispanics as "fucking animals." But they were human, Benton thought. They bled and hurt like all of us. His attitude on this was another thing Benton didn't advertise.

He went back and sat by the desk.

He thought about his conversation with Gold.

A black witch doctor with blue eyes?

Very weird.

Benton didn't know what to think.

The coincidence, though, was notable. The man threatened to kill them, and then one of them died.

He had an idea.

He picked up the phone and dialed the number.

"Medical examiner's office."

"Is Dr. Onairuts there? This is George Benton."

Twenty seconds later, Onairuts came on the phone. "Hey, George, how you doing?"

"Okay, Vic, how are you? Have you been able to stay away from the butts?"

"No problem," Onairuts said. "I keep thinking of the last brand I had before I quit—Cambridge. If I didn't stop I would have died of an inguinal hernia from trying to drag on them."

Benton laughed. "Vic, I wanted to fill you in on this Rivera case."

"You still on that?"

"Yeah," Benton said. "There's a loose end." And then he filled Onairuts in.

"You think there's something else there?"

"I don't know." Benton took a deep breath. "But I was thinking that maybe you should do a more comprehensive autopsy."

"You mean like out at Good Sam?"

Onairuts was referring to the case on Long Island where a male nurse had been charged with killing over a dozen patients by injecting Pavulon, a muscle relaxant, into their systems. Ordinary autopsy wouldn't uncover such a method of murder.

"I thought of that," Benton said, "but the one that first came to mind was Dr. X."

"Ah, yes. Dr. X."

Dr. X was the name given to a doctor in a Jersey hospital where patients also turned up dead. After a number of

55

sophisticated tests, it was determined that they had been poisoned by curare, a virtually undetectable substance.

But Benton well knew that isolating sophisticated poison was difficult and time-consuming, and he would not have been surprised if Onairuts had balked.

"Well, George, I don't like the idea at all, but I can do it. If your instinct tells me to do it, I'll do it."

"We'll have to get a court order to exhume," Benton said.

"Not at all," Onairuts said.

"Why not?"

"Because that wise old owl Onairuts kept tissue and fluid samples in anticipation of something like this. I wasn't satisfied with the results either, and I figured that just maybe you would want something like this done somewhere down the line."

Benton felt a warmth, and a sense of pride. Of all the things in his life, being a detective was the most rewarding.

"That's great," he said.

"Now it will take me only a week to get the results back to you instead of two."

"That's all right. I really appreciate it," Benton said.

"I know you do, George. I know."

CHAPTER 14

The next morning, Benton made arrangements to see Herb Kellner at one that afternoon.

The offices of H.K. Associates were in Manhattan, at 21st Street and Fifth Avenue. The building was a far cry from the glass box that housed Gold and Wishbone Properties. It was a holdover from an older New York, a big granite building with all kinds of fancy trim and big metal double-hung windows.

The long, high-ceilinged lobby featured marble flooring and ornate moldings and mirrors. The elevators were old-fashioned too, featuring metal pointers instead of lighted numbers.

Before going upstairs, Benton did what he always did: he checked the floor directory to see what kinds of companies were in the building. You never knew what meaningful relationships you might spot.

They were mostly garment manufacturers. In fact, he recognized some of the brands.

When he got off the elevator there were six offices,

each with a door that was half wood and half frosted glass with the name of the firm printed in old-fashioned lettering.

There were men's and women's bathrooms on the floor; the floor itself had a bathroom-disinfectant smell.

H.K. Associates was down the hall to the right.

Benton went in and was greeted by a heavyset woman who looked to be about sixty-five. She was about as polished as a dump truck.

Benton identified himself. Respect for the cops was obvious in the woman's entire demeanor.

She led Benton through a narrow hall to Kellner's office, a spare place featuring a metal desk and some metal filing cabinets. The only sign of modernity was the telephone console on the desk.

Kellner smiled nervously, got up from his desk, and shook Benton's hand. His hand was damp. Kellner himself looked nervous. He was tall, thin, balding, and his face was crisscrossed with worry lines.

"Please sit down," he said, and then sat back down behind his desk. "How can I help?"

His voice was high, almost effeminate.

"I was wondering about the visit you were paid at Amalfi's a month ago," Benton said.

Benton thought that a little color had gone out of Kellner's cheeks.

"You think he had something to do with Joe's death?"

Benton thought, this guy is really afraid. "No I don't," he said. "But I do have to investigate."

Kellner's face screwed up. He looked puzzled and anxious at the same time. "I thought the doctor didn't find anything."

"Well, he didn't. Not on first examination. But he's going to run some other tests."

"Oh."

"Could you tell me what happened that night?" Benton asked.

"Oh. Yes."

Kellner detailed the witch doctor's visit to their table, but the difference between his telling of the story and Gold's was like night and day. Gold's general attitude was blasé; Kellner's was fearful, his eyes flitting, his brow knitting as he summoned up images from that night.

But it was essentially the same story, except for one detail.

"He told us he'd stop our hearts," Kellner said.

Gold had just said that the witch doctor said he would kill them.

"He definitely said he would stop your hearts? Those were his words?"

"Yes."

"You're sure?"

"You don't forget something like that."

"Were you contacted after that?" Benton asked.

"Yes. Just a few days ago. At my *home*. That scared me—my number's unlisted."

Benton asked Kellner what the witch doctor had said.

"'Give back Parcel 19 or your heart will be stopped.' That was it."

"Why would someone be so concerned about Parcel 19?"

"No reason," Kellner said. "No reason at all. We bought it three years ago—and nothing has been done with it. I'll tell you, if this thing is haunted, the heck with it. I'd get rid of it."

"How much did you pay for it?"

"We each put in $125,000. We'd get that back pretty easily."

Benton said nothing for a moment. Then: "Did this witch doctor tell you how to contact him?"

"No."

"Okay. If this guy calls you again, give me a ring, will you?" Benton handed Kellner his card.

"You think he will?"

"I don't know. But I don't think he's a real witch doctor. Maybe there's a little scam going on."

"I thought of that," Kellner said. "But what's the scam?"

"I'm going to try to find out."

CHAPTER 15

Helen Archer was lucky. Her call to 911 had pulled two of the best emergency service guys in the city, Hector Lopes and Johnny Wisdom, and they had her in the ambulance, siren screaming, all hooked up to a cardiac monitor machine within eight minutes of her call.

She went flatline once on the way, but Lopes, a five-foot-two Spanish guy whose nickname was "Shane" because of the cool way he operated under intense pressure, had brought her back with a couple of whacks from the defibrillator paddles. She was stable all the rest of the way in.

She stayed in the ICU at Bronx General for three days. She was conscious all the time, and taking nourishment. She had suffered a relatively mild myocardial infarction and was expected to have no further difficulties. She was very happy to have heard from California—from both her daughters. It had a quieting effect on her.

On the fourth day in the hospital she was taken downstairs to a semiprivate room, and she immediately told a nurse that she wanted to talk to a police officer.

"About what, honey?" the nurse asked her.

"About an obscene call that put me here."

The nurse called the 53rd Precinct, the message was taken, and the next day Barbara Babalino was standing next to Mrs. Archer's bed. Mrs. Archer's doctor had said that she could speak with Barbara for fifteen minutes.

Barbara identified herself, then said, "I'm sorry about this. Can you tell me what happened?"

Mrs. Archer detailed what had happened up to the point where she had lost consciousness.

"Okay," Barbara said. "Did the voice sound familiar at all?"

"Yes."

"You know it?"

"No. But it sounded familiar."

"In other words, like you heard it before, but it's not the voice of a friend or relative."

"That's right. Like maybe it was a voice I've heard on TV or the radio."

Barbara paused. She wanted to be careful not to upset Mrs. Archer too much.

"How did he find out about my daughter?" Mrs. Archer asked. "How did he know her name?"

"Well, that's one of the things we're going to be looking into. And as soon as we find out, you'll know."

"That's what really bothers me. If he just called me out of the blue, I wouldn't be so disturbed. But his knowing about me really bothers me."

"You're not the only one he's called, you know."

"No, I didn't know. That makes me feel a little better. How many others?"

"Over twenty years—a lot."

"Do you think he'll call again?"

"If he follows his regular pattern, no. But he may. If he does, there are things you can do."

Barbara then proceeded to give Mrs. Archer the same tips she had given Mrs. Fontana.

"And if he does call, you call me right away."

"I sure will."

Barbara left. She hoped Mrs. Archer wouldn't have to call.

CHAPTER 16

Barbara's anger was building as she headed back to the station house from the hospital; this last call could have killed someone. But she knew she had to control herself. If she said the wrong thing to Bledsoe, or projected an I-told-you-so attitude, she wouldn't get what she was after. Bledsoe always made sure he had the last word.

By the time she entered the station house, around ten-thirty, she had gotten control of herself; all her anger was banked up inside and held in check for now.

Fletcher, Bledsoe's oily aide, was sitting at the desk outside Bledsoe's office.

"I'd like to see the Captain."

Fletcher eyed her up and down, his dark brown eyes undressing her. One day, she thought, she was going to pull her .38 and stick it up his nose.

She pretended not to notice he was being a swine.

Fletcher picked up the phone. "Detective Babalino would like to see you, sir."

Bledsoe glanced up. He immediately adopted a bored

expression. What the fuck now? the expression said. He was so busy doing a crossword puzzle, why let police business interfere?

Barbara went in. "Sir, we had some bad luck with that caller."

"What's that?" Bledsoe asked.

"He called a woman with a heart condition—and he upset her so much she had an attack."

"Serious?"

"She's at ICU in Bronx General. They think she'll live."

There was a pause. Barbara watched Bledsoe's eyes flit around the room as he figured how this could hurt him.

"Sir, I think it's time we did something about this guy —before he kills someone."

"But Babalino," Bledsoe said, "he hasn't killed anyone yet. That's the point. There are people you've been dealing with who have."

Barbara nodded. She was sizzling. This fuck! "You know what I'm afraid of, sir?"

"What?"

"The press getting onto this."

"Why? How are they going to find out?"

"I don't know. How did they find out about Watergate? That started as a misdemeanor."

Bledsoe looked at her. Barbara's face was bland, but she knew that she had made her point. Bledsoe couldn't be sure she wouldn't make a call herself. In the precinct she had a reputation for being something of a nut—she would go off on her own: If that wasn't bad enough, she was engaged to Joe Lawless, a very tough dude.

"If they ever got hold of this," Barbara added, "they could do a number on us."

Bledsoe looked at her with flat eyes. She could tell he was fuming inside. He thought she was working him, but he couldn't be sure about her. This was a woman who could cry about addicts—she was capable of anything.

"All right," he said. "Take some freakin' time and go

after this hump. Christ! We got a precinct full of killers, drug dealers, rapists, burglars—and we're spending time going after obscene telephone callers."

Barbara did everything she could to control a horse-laugh. "Yes, sir," she said, and left.

CHAPTER 17

After talking with Bledsoe, Barbara put out a request to all precincts for other complaints on Dr. Sergeant over the last year.

Over a three-day period they flowed in. At the end of the third day she had computer printouts on 123 of them in the five boroughs. Even without close examination she could see that Sergeant was changing his M.O.

She commandeered a meeting room, closed and locked the door, and sat down to examine them.

After an hour or so, Barbara could see the patterns very clearly.

Usually he would call during the day—the time, Barbara figured, when he thought he was most likely to get a woman home alone answering the phone.

Until very recently, the females he called didn't fit any particular profile. There were complaints from young women, old ones, black, white, oriental—everyone.

On the last three calls reported, the women were all white and in their early fifties.

Also, the three calls were a week apart; in the past they had come in clusters at sporadic times.

The printout didn't have details of the calls' contents, but Barbara knew from recent complaints at the Five Three that she had heard about from other cops that the calls were becoming more vicious. In the past, he would merely call, identify himself as Dr. Sergeant, engage the female in obscene conversation, and hang up. Now he would go through the scam of having kidnapped a relative.

Barbara wondered how many other women he had done this to.

In no case so far had he called anyone twice.

Barbara remembered what Mrs. Archer had said: the voice sounded familiar. Maybe he knew the victims.

Barbara completed examining the material at around eleven o'clock.

She intended to go right home—she hoped Joe would be there.

This time—between ten and two—was the least safe for civilians and cops, the darkest hours of the night, the time when the streets of Siberia were filled with dangerous people.

It was dangerous to cops for another reason. Many on the four-to-twelve tours would do what cops called "four to fours"—the regular tour and then four hours of drinking or dating between male and female partners. It was the main reason that the divorce rate among male members of the force was 50 percent and among female members, close to a mind-boggling 100 percent.

Barbara and Joe weren't married yet, but that wasn't going to happen to them. She knew that cheating on her wasn't in his character, and it certainly wasn't in hers.

She packed the readouts away in a cabinet in her office and then left the station house. As she exited by the front entrance, two uniformed guys—Les Shea and Art Maginnis—were bringing in a black guy who looked to be about nine feet tall. He was shoeless and shirtless, and his head was covered with blood, which had dribbled down onto his face.

"Have a nice evening," Maginnis said to Barbara.

Siberia, she thought. No place like it in the world.

CHAPTER 18

Barbara was feeling chirpy and refreshed when she woke up the next morning. When Lawless had gotten home he had gently awakened her. It had taken her about three minutes to change from a sleepy lady to a sex fiend.

He was gone when she got up, but he had left a note on the kitchen table:

Dear Barbara,

Love,
Joe

Barbara smiled. Among cops and perps alike Joe had a reputation for being a hard guy. And he could be. She remembered way-back-when when she had first met him. She was being threatened with blackmail by a pimp who had spotted some pictures she had posed for in a girlie magazine. It was during a desperate period of her life when she was helping to support her husband, who was a drug addict.

Barbara didn't know what to do or where to turn. But

very calmly and quietly Joe had said that he would talk to the pimp about what he was doing. He did, and the blackmail attempts stopped. Later she learned that Joe had told the pimp that if he didn't stop the blackmail, Joe would have a detective friend fly in from Detroit and clip him.

She sometimes wondered if Joe would actually have done that. The pimp certainly had believed it.

He could do that, yet there was a soft part to him that she loved. He cared. That was Joe. He cared. About her, his job, his fellow cops.

She showered and dressed, then sat at the kitchen table with a cup of tea. The early December sun streamed in the window. Outside, a light snow had whitened the streets and the grass and trees of Pelham Bay Parkway. The holidays were coming. She and Joe would visit her parents . . . it would be a good time.

Her mind flicked to Dr. Sergeant.

During the night, sometime before Joe came home, Barbara had an idea. And as soon as she got into the station house she was going to widen the investigation.

She made the first call from her office at a little after nine.

Yvonne Parker, who worked in the 2nd Precinct out in Nassau, came on the line, and Barbara said hello. She had met Yvonne a few years earlier at a joint NYPD-NCPD conference.

"Hey, Barbara Babalino. How you doin'?"

"Fine. How are you, Yvonne. How's the family?"

"Good. How's Steve?" Yvonne had met Joe Lawless two years ago, and thought he bore a close resemblance to the late actor Steve McQueen.

"Good."

"Hey, you're setting records for longevity. If you ever get tired of that beautiful blond boy, I know a sexy black lady who'd be willing to take him under her wing."

"He's a guy who's hard to get tired of."

"I'll bet," Yvonne said.

"Listen, Yvonne, we've got a real nasty obscene caller who calls and says he's a 'Dr. Sergeant.' I was wondering if you could do some checking for me and see if anyone has made complaints out there recently."

"I never heard of him," Yvonne said, "but I'll check it out."

"Thanks."

"What's your number?"

Barbara gave it to her.

"I should be able to get back to you by the end of the day."

Next Barbara made a call to Frank Ryan. He had been a wire man for the NYPD but had retired and now was doing the same thing for Suffolk. Barbara had known him from when they were first at the Six Two in Brooklyn.

She made the same request of him, and he too said he would get back to her by the end of the day. The name had struck a vague bell with him.

Barbara considered calling Jersey, but then decided not to. There were many different towns in Jersey, each with its own police force. It would mean a lot of calling, and she only had contacts in certain towns. The same was true of Connecticut. Anyway, if there were complaints in Nassau or Suffolk, she could assume there were complaints in Jersey and Connecticut.

Barbara devoted most of the rest of the day to other business: a woman had come in to make a complaint against an ex-boyfriend on a rape charge.

Barbara took the complaint and had the woman examined by a doctor—there was evidence of recent sexual relations—but she wondered how valid the charge was. Just two weeks earlier the complainant's mother had come in to report that she had been raped by an unknown assailant. Small world.

She handled a woman's complaint that her husband beat her. Another woman wanted to get an order of protection to keep her husband away from her.

Then Barbara took a complaint that would earn a high "yuk! factor" from the Siberia cops. A woman had come in to complain that her boyfriend had put a pigeon in a cage —with a pit bull terrier.

At about two o'clock Barbara was about to go to lunch when the phone rang. It was Yvonne.

"Hey, Barbara," Yvonne said. "Dr. Sergeant is working us, too. Over the last six months we got forty complaints on him."

"Who is he calling?"

"Anybody who wears a skirt."

"What are the most recent?"

Yvonne gave them to her, and they fit the new pattern: two calls, both a week apart, the first one seven weeks earlier. Both were to women in their early fifties, one in Mineola, the other in New Hyde Park. Before those two the complainants had been different ages, nationalities, etc. Barbara was willing to bet that Dr. Sergeant was getting nastier with the last two women than those before.

She got the addresses of the complainants from Yvonne.

"We have to get together soon," Barbara said.

"Well, if not you—then just send blondie."

They laughed.

Frank Ryan called an hour later.

There had been a cluster of complaints against Dr. Sergeant in the last year—over fifty.

But the last two were the same profile as those in Nassau—calls to women in their early fifties, and they had occurred four and five weeks ago. Counting the calls in the city, and Nassau, he had contacted seven different women in their early fifties, one a week, over the past seven weeks.

His victim profile had changed. The question was why. And what would he do next?

CHAPTER 19

Around eleven o'clock at night, three days after she had met with Lawless, Magee, and Jerry, Francie Collins went into the 592 Club bar. She had been alerted by an undercover cop from the DA's office who had been hanging out there that Charlie McCoy had come in.

Francie had been getting ready every night, and she walked out the door ten minutes after she got the call. She was all dolled up and wore a low-cut dress that would draw male eyes like a magnet. A Kel recorder was in her bag.

The 592 Club was a typical Bronx bar that had been converted to club status—it now had live bands and a space for dancing.

It was a fairly long room. On the right as you came in was the bar, directly opposite it was the bandstand, and in between were tables and space for dancing. In the rear were more tables and dancing space.

The patrons of the club, in a borough that was predominantly black and Hispanic, were all white, mostly Irish-

American, with more than a few donkeys—pure Irish. Most of the patrons did not live in the area but traveled in, particularly Fridays and Saturdays, for drinking, dancing, and listening to bands who played a mix of Irish, country, and rock songs.

On the door and window to the 592 Club were signs that said MEMBERS ONLY. There was no formal membership in the club, but blacks and Hispanics understood what the signs meant.

Francie went to the crowded bar, slipped in between two guys, and ordered a drink. She had spotted Charlie as soon as she came in. He was in the rear, sitting at a table with another guy. Francie did nothing to indicate that she saw him, though she thought he saw her.

The music from the band behind her—they were playing "Blueberry Hill"—was so loud that she could feel her lungs vibrate. The recorder was off; any conversation with this background noise wouldn't be heard anyway. She wanted badly to get something. Maybe one night's work could be worth twenty fucking large!

She finished her drink within a minute and ordered another. It was easy to drink now. She was nervous. Charlie was a little crazy. There was no telling what he would do if he found the wire.

The band had stopped, and the leader announced they would take a break.

Before the next drink came, one of the guys standing next to her turned and looked her up and down—but mostly down. "Who are you, baby?" he said.

"None of your fucking business."

The guy blinked and turned away.

It took a while before the bartender came up with Francie's second drink and set it down.

"I'll take care of that," a voice behind her said.

She turned and looked surprised, though she knew who it was. "Hey, Charlie," she said. "How are you?"

"Good. What are you doing here?"

"It's a long story."

Francie turned back to the bar and took her drink. She sipped it, then turned and faced Charlie. Her tits were a foot from his chest.

"I'm sorry to hear about Jerry."

"Thank you."

"Are you waiting for somebody?"

"No. I was feeling kind of shitty, so I just thought I'd come back to a place where me and Jerry used to have a lot of fun."

"Oh. Yeah. Yeah. Sorry about that. Sorry about that."

Francie looked at him. Charlie was crazy to begin with, but he was also using. The black pupils of his light blue eyes looked like twin Holland Tunnels.

Francie said nothing.

"You want to join me and Mike?" Charlie asked. "We're sitting in back."

"I don't know." Francie smiled. "I don't know what I want to do."

Francie caught Charlie sneaking a look at her chest, but she hid her reaction.

"C'mon. You should be with friends, right?"

"Right," Francie said.

She finished her drink, and Charlie led her to the back. As she walked she reached into her bag.

Fifteen minutes later, Francie and McCoy were sitting alone at the table way in the back. Five minutes after she had gone back to the table she had seen Charlie give Mike —she didn't know who the fuck he was—the eye so he could be there alone with her. That was okay with her.

She had another drink and noticed that Charlie was getting more whacked. She was a little worried. He got crazier when he drank and popped pills. "Hey, Charlie," she said. "I got to get the fuck out of here. This noise is fucking killing me."

"Where you going?"

"For a walk. I don't know."

"I'll come with you."

Francie had no objection.

From the 592 Club they walked across Kingsbridge Road and into Poe Park. There had been a lot of small talk at the table. She had to make a move.

"So how you doin'?" Francie said.

"I'm doin' okay."

"Really. The word I got was that Jimmy really fucked you."

Charlie was quiet. Then: "All I did for that fuck. You know what I did for that bag of shit?"

"I know. Everybody knows. Jerry says that no one was a friend of Jimmy's like you was."

"Fuckin' A."

"That you were at his back in a lot of shit."

"Fuckin' A right. I remember after we whacked the Diamond . . ."

Excitement screamed through the pleasant haze the whiskey had produced in Francie. "Oh yeah, I remember," she said. "You was called out by the wops to Brooklyn to explain."

"Fuckin' A. Jimmy comes up to me and says, 'The wops called a meeting in Brooklyn. I got to go out there. I think they're going to kill me because we clipped the Diamond. I was wondering if you wanted to come with me.'

"I said I was comin', right? So me and Jimmy drove out there one night to Bravato's, a big guinea restaurant in Bay Ridge, right? And they tell us not to bring no fucking guns to the meeting. You bring a gun and that's enough to get you killed. So Jimmy has two guns on him, and so do I."

Charlie stopped. He reached into his pocket, popped a pill.

Francie sat down on a bench. Charlie sat next to her. Francie put the pocketbook down between them. "Then what happened?"

"Yeah," Charlie said. "We get there and outside in the

bar, before we go into the back room, we see Roy DiNatale, who Jimmy knew from the joint, and he warned us that whatever we say we shouldn't admit we whacked the Diamond.

"We didn't," Charlie continued, "and we were questioned by them guineas—there was a real rogue's gallery of about ten guineas back there, including Paul Capotosto, the big cheese. We managed to bullshit our way out, but from that time on they started demanding ten percent of everything and one percent vig on all loans. But from that time on, too, I was Jimmy's right-hand man. I stood behind that bag of shit many a time."

"And you got shot, too, didn't you?"

"Fuckin' A, the night we iced Calhoun, the union guy. He had a fucking ex-Green Beret guarding him. We had to take him out too. But that fucker shot me in the left hand—I still don't have complete use of it."

Charlie held up his hand and showed her that he could only move three fingers.

He suddenly turned to her. Something gripped her stomach, but then it was okay.

"Hey," he said. "I don't think he did too good by Jerry, either, right? I got word that he wasn't taking care of you while Jerry was in the slammer."

"I never heard from the fuck."

Charlie nodded. "Hey, you okay now?"

"I guess."

"Want another drink?"

"Sure."

"Come to my place. I still live around here."

"Why not?" she said.

CHAPTER 20

Charlie lived up on 233rd Street and Bailey Avenue in a three-room apartment on the second floor. Bailey was still one of the white neighborhoods, but Charlie really didn't give a fuck what it was: he was almost always packing, and he would take care of any trouble real quick.

Francie had been at Charlie's apartment once before, about two years earlier. Then it was neat and clean; now everything looked broken and worn down. Just goes to show you, she thought, what being loyal to a scumbag can get you.

Before they made love, she carefully guided Charlie to talk about three more murders that he and Toolan had done.

She was worried, before they fucked, if she was going to be able to get wet. But it was no problem. Charlie, despite being whacked, was a good lover, and all she had to do when he was fucking her was imagine he was Jerry. The booze helped. She even was able to suck him off.

It was a little embarrassing to know that the fuzz would be listening to this, but they didn't say much, just made sounds. Then it was over and they were sitting in the bed together.

Francie figured she had enough. It was time to leave.

"You're some woman," Charlie said.

"I'm glad I ran into you, Charlie."

"Yeah, me too."

They were quiet for a time. Francie toyed with the idea of getting more out of Charlie. But years of street experience told her no. She had gotten a lot. And Charlie was from the streets too. He might wonder why all they talked about between fucking was murder. She had a blade with her, but if he went into her bag she would be in real trouble.

She pulled the covers back and stood up. She was completely nude. Charlie's eyes were on her tits. He was in dreamland.

"I got to be going," she said.

"Why don't you stay the night?"

"I can't. My mother's watching the kids, and I got to get back."

"Do you think I could see you again?"

"Sure," Francie said. "You'll see me again."

And she thought: Charlie was not a bad guy. It was too bad she had to do this to him. But Jerry was her husband, and there was nothing she wouldn't do to save him and her kids. That was it.

A few minutes later, Francie was on the street. It was a little before one o'clock. It was cold. She sucked in some deep breaths to clear her head.

If she didn't have to be wired anymore, she would have done quite well. She had spent two hours with Charlie. That was ten large an hour. It beat getting rent money from her mother.

CHAPTER 21

Within twelve hours after Francie Collins had met with Charlie McCoy, the taped conversations had been transcribed and Delano Magee, Lawless, and Mary Lee Baxter were discussing them in her office.

"What do you think, Mary Lee?" Magee asked.

"Very good. I think that when we hit McCoy with this he's going to fall—and take people with him. You've got Collins, McCoy, Sheehan, Curran, Caulfield, Leone, and other Bronxies working for Toolan on drugs, loansharking, murder—you've got a solid case against Toolan and at least four of the other Bronxies. I'm sure some will flip, which will make the cases excellent."

"When do you want to collar McCoy?" Lawless asked.

"We have the possibility of a safe house now for Francie, but I wanted you to look it over to make sure it's okay. As you know, we've got Jerry in Leavenworth for safekeeping. I think as soon as we get Francie and her kids in the safe house we can bring Jerry up and bust Charlie after that."

"When will that be?" Lawless asked.

"Maybe day after tomorrow."

"Good," Magee said.

"Where's McCoy now?" Mary Lee asked.

"Doing his usual routines. We've got him under surveillance."

Mary Lee, who had been sitting behind her desk, stood up. She eyed the pretzel tin, then looked away. "The only thing we could use that we don't have here is some physical corroboration of the crimes, or at least one of them. I realize that's difficult to get, but . . ."

"What I plan to do," Lawless said, "is to study the transcripts. We'll just pick the best lead and follow it."

"I know it's going to be tough, Joe. None of the homicides either Collins or McCoy talked about are fresh. Jim is going to be looking them over too, right?"

Jim was Jim Ferguson, the FBI agent heading the federal team on the investigation.

"Right. I talked with him about them."

"Good," Mary Lee said.

There was a pause.

"And what are you going to be doing, Del?" Mary Lee asked. "You've got nothing to do."

"I'm going to be praying," Magee said. "Praying it all turns out all right."

And they all laughed.

CHAPTER 22

It seemed that Barbara and Lawless would always each get home when the other was asleep. But the day Lawless spoke with Mary Lee Baxter he and Barbara arrived home at the same time. Lawless had been studying the transcripts with Ferguson, the FBI agent, while Barbara had been trying to handle all her other squeals in addition to the obscene telephone caller.

They made tea and sat in the kitchen.

"One good thing about this job," Lawless said. "It's got a diet plan better than Weight Watchers."

"What'd you eat today?"

"A slice of pizza and a cup of coffee. And you?"

"Four cups of coffee, three cups of tea, and a donut."

"Terrific."

"You want something, Joe?"

"I'm full."

Barbara laughed.

Lawless lit a cigarette. Barbara, he thought, was a good

actress. She didn't give any hint of disliking his smoking, but he knew she did.

"So how you doing on Dr. Sergeant?" Lawless asked.

"Nothing yet. I'm trying to find a link among the women, but I haven't yet. I just have so much time in the day. There's something there, but I can't quite get a handle on it."

"Keep whacking. You know what being a detective is like, right?"

It had been compared to the life of a miner. Sometimes you had to move a mountain of earth to find one nugget.

"How's with you, Joe?"

Lawless almost hesitated. Long experience had shown him that when somebody's life was dependent on people keeping things to themselves you had to be extremely careful. Some people couldn't keep a secret.

But Barbara wasn't that way, and he felt he could talk with her about the Toolan case, though, as much as he loved and respected her, he might stop short of telling her exactly where the safe house would be. It wasn't that he didn't trust her. He did. Call it superstition.

"I've been studying the transcript of the recording Francie and Charlie McCoy made."

He took a drag on his cigarette.

"We got a lot of good stuff to bring down other Bronxies, and we've got Toolan tied into four homicides. He killed one guy in a bar on 73rd Street. Knew the guy slightly. They were drinking, and the guy said Toolan's brother seemed like a fag to him.

"They went downstairs at one point to take a leak, and McCoy says that while standing at the urinal next to this guy Toolan took out a .32 and blew his brains all over the room. They just left the body there. There were guys in the bar who knew Toolan, and they heard the shot, but nobody said anything. They knew better.

"We've also got him tied into an execution of a rogue drug dealer for the Family—this is a guy Toolan was godfather to one of his kids—and another killing of an ex-buddy of his who Toolan thought had sided with another gang leader. They took that guy out to a Queens cemetery, and the guy swore up and down that he was Toolan's friend and that if he didn't believe that, well—he handed Toolan his own gun and said shoot me—and Toolan did, then drove back and forth over him with his car until he was chopped meat."

"Psycho."

"Yeah. Collins says he thinks Toolan may have clipped over a hundred guys, starting when he was running loose on the streets at age twelve."

Lawless crushed his cigarette out.

"But I got one that we're especially going to look into. It's the murder of Benny Iannelo, a small-time hood. It happened about four years ago, according to Collins and McCoy. Benny owed Toolan a big seven hundred bucks and didn't pay up, so Toolan lured him to an apartment on Valentine off Fordham and shot him in the head with a twenty-two automatic. Then, to make sure he was dead—and to make sure that Collins and McCoy were involved, as well as another guy named Vito Tassone whose apartment it was—Toolan commanded each of them to stab Benny in the heart. They did, then they cut him up in the tub, packaged the parts in plastic, and dumped them in the river. But Toolan walked around with Benny's head for a while. Toolan likes to send messages to people."

Barbara refilled Lawless's tea. "So why is it promising?"

"Listen to this."

Lawless went out of the room for a moment and returned with a transcript.

"This is from the transcript of the wire on McCoy, describing the Benny Ianello killing to Francie: '. . . he gave us no idea he was to,' it's garbled or inaudible in places, 'that little fuck . . . but I didn't care. I still,' garbled, 'for that bag of shit. Me and Vito stabbed Benny in the heart

85

right there on the fucking board floor...he bled like a stuck pig...and totally fucking...' etcetera.

"I checked it out," Lawless continued. "The building is still standing. I'm hoping that no one did any improvements on it. Maybe a little of the blood seeped down into the floorboards. Maybe we can get a little corroboration."

"Good idea," Barbara said.

"We're gong to try. You never know."

"Good luck."

Lawless drained the last of his tea. "Good luck to you, sweetie. Let's go to bed. To sleep."

"You got that right."

And they laughed.

CHAPTER 23

The next day, Lawless spent most of the morning obtaining a warrant to search the third-floor apartment, 3B, at 2378 Valentine Avenue.

Meanwhile Jerry Collins was being brought back from Leavenworth. He arrived at noon.

At around two o'clock, everything was in place. Jim Ferguson and a couple of his guys were to accompany Lawless and two of his detectives and a forensic man to the address. Lawless had a tape recorder with him.

One of the Siberia detectives was Arnold Gertz. Gertz wasn't the best of investigators, but in this situation, where you had to guard somebody, or maybe break down a door, or tranquilize somebody, he was without peer, the ultimate in muscle.

Lawless and the prosecutors knew they were taking a couple of chances bringing Collins to the apartment.

For one thing, on the street he could always try something stupid, like making a break for it. In Collins's case this was highly unlikely—he had everything to lose and little to gain—but it was difficult to figure what a criminal would do in any particular set of circumstances. It was important to follow your own procedures, which would control what the criminal might want to do.

A greater and more real danger was Collins being spotted by someone who knew Toolan and reporting that he saw him on the street with the cops. Valentine Avenue, like other streets in Siberia, was infested with drugs, and it was highly likely that someone on the street would know Toolan. Whether they knew Toolan *and* Collins was another question. Lawless knew that dealers and addicts would recognize him and his squad.

They were in luck. The sky, which had been powder blue, and sunny, suddenly turned gray, dark clouds formed, and by twenty after two it was raining hard in the Bronx, a typical cold December rain which would drive everyone indoors.

When Lawless arrived at Valentine Avenue, the street was rainswept and empty.

To further minimize the chance of exposure, they pulled up to the house in a battered van.

Like others on both sides of the block, the house was red brick and six stories high. Once, Lawless knew, the building had housed typical middle-class families that had been the backbone of the city. But they had long ago fled to the suburbs, leaving the buildings to deteriorate and ultimately die.

Also like the other buildings on the block, 2378 was abandoned. At one time all of the windows had been fitted with painted sheet metal covers, but half of these had been torn out, even high up. The vandals couldn't let anything stand.

Equipped with twelve-battery flashlights, and with Collins cuffed only behind his back, they entered the building quickly.

There was no one there.

The foyer was littered with empty crack vials, assorted

needles, crushed cigarette butts. Graffiti included two scrawled *Fuck you*s, one in English, the other in Spanish.

Lawless worried that the stairs might not be intact. But they were. They were to the right, through another doorway.

The light got worse as they climbed the stairs; flashlights were needed.

As they climbed, they heard things moving ahead of and beneath them: rats. All of these abandoned buildings were inhabited by rats and mice, who coexisted, Lawless had once learned, because their feeding habits were different.

The first-floor landing also had a few crack vials. There were none on the second and third, but the graffiti continued.

Gertz had with him a wrecking bar and some other tools, but he didn't need them to open the door, which was made of heavy metal and was already bowed in the middle and open when they arrived. How that happened was anyone's guess.

"Yeah," Collins said. "This is the place. I remember."

"Lead the way."

They pushed the door open. It was jet black inside.

Flashlight beams probed the darkness: a rat, eyes red in the light, scurried away.

Down the hall was a bathroom; the end of the toilet could be seen.

They walked the hall. To the right was a kitchen.

"Happened in the living room," Collins said.

They went further down the hall. Directly in front was the bathroom.

All the windows in the living room were plugged. It was simply too dark to see.

"Peel back one of those windows, will you Arnold?"

"Sure, Joe."

Gertz used the wrecking bar to get under a corner of the window, gripped the corner with his hand, and tore the rectangle of sheet metal out with a shearing sound. Then he took another out.

Gray light flooded the room. There were scurrying sounds in the walls. Rain slanted in.

Lawless looked around. There was nothing much except broken plaster, rodent droppings, and the characteristic grease marks rats who were almost blind made when they used the baseboards to guide themselves across a room.

Lawless went over to Collins and removed his cuffs. "Where'd it happen, Jerry?"

"Over here," he said. "I didn't expect it, and neither did Vito. Toolan was telling Benny that he shouldn't have tried to fuck him out of the seven hundred bucks. Benny was real scared. He said he wasn't trying to fuck him, because he knew how Toolan was. And they were sort of circling, and then there was a loud *pop* and I saw Benny go down. Jimmy had shot him once in the head."

Collins stepped over to a spot in the middle of the room.

"Then when he was down he looked dead—you know, blood was jetting from him like from a hose—and Jimmy said to get a kitchen knife and for me and Vito to stab him in the heart to make sure he was dead. So we did, and then we took him into the bathroom and put him into the tub. Vito and Jimmy cut him up and put him in black plastic and then took him out and threw him into the Bronx River. That was it."

"Lot of blood here?" Ferguson asked.

"A fucking lake. But we cleaned it up."

"Arnold, you got that cat's paw?" Lawless asked.

"Yeah, Joe, I do."

Gertz produced a short crowbar-like tool called a cat's paw that was especially designed for removing floorboards.

Carefully Arnold pried up the nails that held the floor in place, then used a hammer to pull the nails and lift the boards one by one.

Lawless's pulse accelerated. The edges of one of the tongue-and-grooved boards had dark stains on it.

90

Heidt, the forensic guy, didn't need to be told. He got down and used a small knife to scrape some of the darkened material off the edges of the boards into a thin plastic pouch.

"Blood?" Lawless said.

"Bet on it," Heidt answered.

As Gertz removed each of the boards in turn, more and more material was scraped into the pouch. After a few minutes it looked like flakes of tobacco.

"We got enough," Heidt said.

Lawless had been distracted by Heidt's actions. He looked at Collins. Collins was looking at the wall between the two windows.

"What's up, Jerry?" Lawless asked.

"The bullet," Collins said. "I remember it went through Benny's head and into the wall."

"Really? Are you sure?" Lawless asked. Normally, a bullet fired from a .22 wouldn't go through a human head unless it was powered by additional powder—a magnum load.

But executions were usually done with a normal powder load just so that the bullet wouldn't exit. It would careen and plow a pinball path through brain matter. That's why killers liked it. A head shot was almost a sure kill, and the .22 made very little noise.

But it could happen. Sometimes the bullet did exit.

"Where did it hit?" Lawless asked.

Collins went over to the wall; Lawless and Heidt followed.

Collins pointed to a spot about three feet from the ceiling. It was a patch, raised and not unlike a series of other patches on the wall—in fact, there were perhaps two dozen, in addition to large cracks that were unrepaired.

Using a knife, Heidt carefully dug into the wall starting on the outside of the patch. It was hard, but it yielded.

He got all the patching material out. There was no bullet.

Next to this patch was another. He repeated the procedure. No one said anything, but just watched him work.

He dug deep, and the plaster cascaded onto the floor.

Three quarters of an inch into the wall he saw something silver.

"See!" Collins said.

Everybody saw it.

Ballistics said the bullet was deformed but could definitely be identified as a .22 slug.

The scrapings taken from the floorboards were mixed with a reagent and the result was conclusive: type O blood, which was, according to the autopsy performed some four years before, the blood type of Benny Ianello.

And there was a bonus. The bullet also showed minute traces of blood—again, type O.

The prosecutors and cops were ecstatic.

Now they had physical evidence that confirmed what both Collins and McCoy had told them independently.

Slowly but surely they were building a nice case against Toolan. And so far there had been no sign that Toolan knew what was going on.

CHAPTER 24

Ostensibly, George Benton did regular tours like everyone else on the NYPD. But regular tours were a fiction in Fort Siberia. There hadn't been a single day since he arrived four years earlier that he had gotten off after just eight hours of work. The only time he got off early was when he thought he was having a coronary or some other vascular accident.

On this day, he got home at about nine o'clock after his theoretical eight to four.

Like Joe Lawless, Benton lived on Pelham Bay Parkway. His apartment was only two blocks from Jacobi Hospital, a massive public facility and one of the better hospitals in the city, attached as it was to the Einstein Teaching College.

Benton had chosen his apartment for its close proximity to the hospital. In the event of his suffering a myocardial infarction the EMS could be at his door in minutes. If he had to, he might even be able to walk there.

The mail held nothing from Beth. Just some junk mail

and bills, which was mostly what he always got.

Disappointed, he climbed the three flights to his four-room apartment and let himself in.

His cat, Alien Nation—so called because of her multicolored fur—was in the living room on one of the windowsills, observing the street, where there were trees—and birds—thinking, Benton assumed, homicidal thoughts.

He went into the bathroom, which was notable for its medicine cabinet. It had been custom-made for Benton by a cop friend who moonlighted as a carpenter.

The cabinet was immense—three feet high, with its ends flush against flanking walls eight feet apart. It was filled with medicines, drugs, potions, and some medical hardware, such as an oxygen tank and a stethoscope. Benton was ready for Armageddon in his body.

A year ago, for his birthday, the squad had somehow obtained a defunct X-ray machine, lovingly wrapped it up, and gave it to him along with a card which said he could now X ray himself before starting each tour. Benton had laughed.

Now he had a headache.

He took out bottles of extra-strength Tylenol, Advil, and aspirin. He drew a glass of water and swallowed the tablets—two of each. If it wasn't a brain tumor, the headache should clear up shortly.

But he wasn't really focused on his headache. When a case gripped him, as this Rivera one was starting to do, he had relatively little anxiety.

Benton went out of the bathroom and into the bedroom. He hung up his jacket, took off his gun and hung it up, took off his pants, hung them up, and lay down on the bed. He could feel his body pulses rhythmically ticking. He had taught himself not to concentrate on pulses to see if they skipped a beat.

He had gone about as far as he could with the Rivera case. What was intriguing was the small amount of time between the warning to Rivera and his death. But no way did Benton believe that a witch doctor had caused Rivera's death. If Rivera was a homicide victim, there was a perp somewhere, and he had nothing to do with voodoo.

Most people would probably have been shocked at Benton's attitude toward the case. He was so eccentric and "bent" they would figure, he would think a witch doctor could do something like this. Not Benton. When it came to police work, he was as rooted in reality as anyone could be.

Yesterday, he had spoken to Frank DeVito, the other partner in the Parcel 19 deal.

DeVito didn't think the witch doctor's visit amounted to "a hill of shit."

"Just some whack," he said, "getting his stones off."

When Benton asked him if he was worried, DeVito said that if the witch doctor fucked with him it was the witch doctor who should be worried.

Benton had also contacted his cousin, Brian Burke, who worked at the Bank of Ireland and had asked him to check the three men and their companies. Benton had no idea what Burke would find, but the more information you had on an investigation the better off you were.

As he lay on the bed, Alien Nation came in, leaped up, and paraded past Benton so he could get a good look at her ass. Sometimes it was more than a look.

Sometimes Benton wondered what parading your ass in someone's face signified. Did that mean that you were confident and sure of yourself—or psychotic?

Benton felt the headache receding.

He got up and went to the closet and put on his robe.

Yes, he was getting a little better. He had no feeling, for example, that he had to carry his gun around the apartment with him. Gurgling, creaking, and other sounds were not necessarily life-threatening.

He went into the kitchen, which, like the other rooms in

the apartment, was spotless. He was so clean that he even changed A.N.'s litter every day.

He fed her a blend of wet and dry food. He was conscious of *her* arteries too. He only wanted to feed her healthy stuff. He once wondered if they could treat cats for MIs.

He went into the living room, turned on the TV, and sat down. The phone rang.

He went into the kitchen and picked up. "Hello."

"Detective Benton?"

"Yes."

"This is Herb Kellner. I just . . . you told me to call. I just got a call from the witch doctor . . . really shook me up."

"What'd he say?"

"He said that I hadn't given up Parcel 19 . . . that it was coming close to the time when he would stop my heart . . . like Rivera. Jesus!"

"Mr. Kellner," Benton said, "there's something going on that we don't know about—but there's no witch doctor."

"What do I do?"

"Take a trip out of town. Stay away from the phone. We'll get to the bottom of this."

"I have a business here." There was a silence. Then, "I . . . I guess I could go away for a few days. I guess I could do that. Maybe I should just forget about Parcel 19."

"I wouldn't do that," Benton said. "Just take that short vacation."

Another pause.

"I will," Kellner said. "I will. Thank you."

"Just tell your secretary how to contact you. Maybe you could set up a signal for calling you."

"Yes, yes. I could do that. I will."

It took Benton only a couple of minutes to reach DeVito at his home in Huntington Hills on Long Island. Benton asked if he had been called.

96

"Yeah," DeVito said, "that hump called me."

"What'd he say?"

"He said if I didn't give up on Parcel 19 he'd stop my pump."

"What'd you say?"

"I told him to go fuck himself and hung up."

"All right."

"You didn't find out nothing yet, huh?" DeVito asked.

"No, but we're looking into it."

"Okay. Be in touch."

They hung up.

It took Benton a half hour before he was able to speak with David Gold. Gold was concerned, but not as frightened as Kellner.

"I mean, we're dealing with a nut here," he said.

"Yes."

"Have you any idea who this guy is?"

"Not yet," Benton said.

There was a pause.

"What are you going to do?" Benton asked.

"I don't know."

CHAPTER 25

Benton called Brian Burke at the Bank of Ireland at nine o'clock the next morning. As it happened, Burke was almost finished with his investigation, and he called Benton back at around ten.

"Anything?" Benton asked.

"Not really," Burke said. "I mean, these guys are not Xerox, but they come up pretty good on their D&B reports. They all have pretty good liquidity."

"Meaning?"

"Well, they have enough cash to pay their bills. Some companies don't—and that's a way you can tell they're in trouble."

"How long do they have to pay before they get a black mark?"

"Thirty days is standard," Burke said. "But one of the companies here, HK Associates, pays on a ten-plus-two basis. That means they pay their bills within ten days, so they're entitled to discount the bills two percent."

"I see."

"Two of the companies are public—Wishbone and De-Vito. Here again, they get good marks."

"Can you send me this stuff fast, Brian."

"I'll send it by messenger."

"Thanks a lot."

After he finished talking with Burke, Benton called On-airuts. He was in.

"How's it going, Vic? Anything yet on those tests?"

"We have some results in. So far everything is negative."

"Hmm," Benton said.

"Another few days and I'll have them all."

"Okay, thanks. How's the antismoking crusade going?"

"Fine. No problem. I just murdered my dog."

Benton laughed.

After he hung up, Benton closed his eyes. Mentally, he reviewed everything he had done so far in the case.

Then he went to the file cabinet and pulled the DD5s he had written.

He reread them.

Nothing. No ideas.

Maybe tomorrow, he thought, after a good night's sleep, he'd take a fresh look. Maybe that would help.

CHAPTER 26

At around seven in the evening the day after the witch doctor called him, Frank DeVito pulled his white Eldorado into the bluestone turnaround outside his $1.2 million home in Huntington Hills, an exclusive section of the town of Huntington.

DeVito planned to do exactly nothing tonight except have some fun with his girlfriend, Linda, who at twenty-three was thirty years his junior but who had trouble keeping up with him sexually.

DeVito was mentally tired. For the past few days he had been putting the final touches on a deal that would get for him and a subsidiary of his firm, RDR Redemption Services, all of the collection work of Philley's, a chain with over 230 department stores up and down the East Coast.

Today he had sealed the deal with promise of a $150,000 payment which was to be deposited over a one-year period into the account of one of the president's sons, who lived in San Francisco. There would be no trail of paper that some energetic bloodhound of a U.S. attorney, like that crazy guinea in the city, could follow.

There was no telling, DeVito thought, how much the deal would be worth. But on its face the contract was for $2 million a year, and it would likely come to at least 3.2.

DeVito got out of the car. As he approached the front door, he took out his keys and looked at the brass plate, mounted on the door, on which the name DeVito was etched in beautiful script.

Somebody, he saw, had smudged it a little.

When he got up close he used the sleeve of his jacket to polish it shiny.

He opened the door and went inside. Immediately, he closed the door and stepped to the right. On the wall was the Wells Fargo open-circuit alarm system. He had ninety seconds to tap in his code. He did so.

The interior of the house had the massive look of the outside, though the ceilings were not high. It was the Mediterranean-style furniture that did it—massive carved pieces, dark walls, gilt-edged frames. It looked like a floor in a museum.

No one was home, nor had anyone been home for two years now, since DeVito's third wife had left, and the only way he knew she was alive was because his alimony checks, sent to a post office box in Las Vegas, were cashed at the Las Vegas Mercantile Bank.

He rarely saw his two daughters, either. Both lived in California and were married. They would occasionally call.

DeVito went into his bedroom, which was up a short flight of wide, carpet-covered steps that led to the second floor.

He went into his bedroom. It featured a canopied bed with a horizontal shade that could be opened by motorization to reveal a mirror. DeVito liked to see himself screwing. Linda liked looking at herself too.

The telephone answering machine, which was on a table near the bed, was on.

He activated the playback and listened. There were ten calls, all about business except one—his housekeeper said she would be in at the regular time the next morning.

DeVito opened the door to a massive closet. A door-length mirror was secured to it.

Carefully, watching himself in the mirror, he stripped, laying things on the bed as he did.

Finally he was nude. He had a little belly but otherwise was in good shape. He was chunky, muscular, and he liked his body hair, which was thick and black—not a strand of gray. He had gotten hair on his balls at the age of ten. It was something he was very proud of. .

He spread his legs apart and fondled his balls. He liked the way they hung down, and their heaviness. He liked the way they made a thumping sound against Linda when he fucked her.

He went into the upstairs bathroom and turned on the shower.

But before he did he noticed something on the wall-to-wall indoor-outdoor carpet. There was a big damp spot.

He knelt down and felt it. He smelled his fingers. It was odorless.

He looked at himself in the mirror. He kept clean-shaven, but his beard, predictably, was heavy. Sometimes he had to shave twice a day.

"I love you, Frank," Linda had said, "but your beard's like sandpaper. You tear me up."

So Frank would shave. He always shaved after a shower when his skin was soft, though it was always softer in the evening than in the morning.

He adjusted the shower spray and temperature, stepped in, and closed the glass door behind him.

As he soaped himself up he thought of the deal with Philley's. It was sweet. And it would probably lead to other contacts.

He stayed in the shower five minutes, then got out.

He dried himself off with a huge towel and then stood in front of the mirror, still nude.

He took a can of shaving cream from the medicine cabinet and carefully soaped his beard up.

He put the can down and pulled up the stopper in the sink and got ready to shave.

Frank's girlfriend, Linda, arrived at the house at eight o'clock.

She wondered why the outside light wasn't on. In fact, there seemed to be only a faint light coming from inside the house.

But Frank was here. His Caddie was parked in the turn-around.

Linda had her own key. She let herself in.

Immediately, she heard the sound of the fan going in the bathroom upstairs.

As she walked into the foyer, she got a damp feeling. It was very humid inside.

Then she saw something that alarmed her. It had darkened almost all the carpet on the steps and a big area of the rug at the base. It was a damn puddle.

Suddenly afraid, Linda picked her way upstairs past the water.

My God, she thought, maybe Frank had an accident.

She got to the bathroom door.

She opened the door. Mist billowed out, and for a moment she couldn't see anything. Then she did. And then she was screaming.

CHAPTER 27

Barbara Babalino had gotten permission from the Nassau and Suffolk PD's to talk to victims of Dr. Sergeant. Not that, strictly speaking, she needed permission. But there could be jealousy and backbiting among departments, and it was the politic thing to do.

Thus far, she had been able to talk to two of the women in Nassau County but without results. Barbara had come to believe that there was some sort of link among the women. But she couldn't determine what it was. No one knew any of the others, and the only thing they had in common was that they were female and in their early fifties.

Interviewing the third woman had added a new element to the mystery. The woman, Alice Smith, had an *unlisted* phone number, yet Dr. Sergeant had called her. And, as with the other victims, he had known the name of Mrs. Smith's daughter.

How did he get such knowledge? Mrs. Smith said that she only gave out the number to her immediate friends and, sometimes, business establishments or government agencies. But that was it.

Barbara's investigation had eaten up several days. Bledsoe was starting to make noise. He wanted to know if she had made any progress. She told him no, but she declined to tell him that the case had spilled over into Nassau and Suffolk and Jersey. Then he would start beefing that the case was out of their jurisdiction.

It was around two weeks before Christmas when Barbara arranged to meet with the final Nassau complainant. The woman lived in a four-story red-brick apartment building in Mineola within walking distance of the Long Island Rail Road station.

It was hard to believe, it occurred to her as she walked, that Mineola was only a half hour from the Bronx. It had clean streets, no graffiti, no broken glass and garbage in the streets, no broken-down abandoned buildings, no broken-down abandoned people.

But Barbara knew Nassau and Suffolk were not Nirvana. The appearance was wonderful, but behind the *Our Town* look she knew there was crime. It was just a matter of degree.

The woman's name was Herrera. Barbara found herself a little nervous. She was going to have to come up with something soon.

Barbara took the elevator to the third floor. As she rode it up, it occurred to her that it was nice to enter an apartment building and not have to worry about perhaps confronting a whacked-out junkie mugger.

Mrs. Herrera answered the door.

Her complaint listed her as fifty-three, but she seemed at least ten years younger. She was blond-haired with only a trace of gray, pretty with few lines, and trim.

But Barbara could tell from a certain slight movement of her eyes that she was nervous. Most people were nervous when talking to cops. Barbara always tried to make herself uncoplike. She wore casual clothes, didn't show her badge, identified herself as Barbara Babalino from the city, and tried to make questioning as conversational as possible.

Mrs. Herrera offered to make tea or coffee, and Barbara accepted. When the tea was finished, they sat in the neat, clean kitchen and talked.

As gently as possible, Barbara elicited from Mrs. Herrera her experience with Dr. Sergeant. It had been the same as the other women—or at least it had started out that way.

He had claimed to have taken her only child, her daughter Janie, and he said that he would harm Janie if Mrs. Herrera didn't do what he wanted her to do.

"I just hung up," she said, "because Janie was sitting right next to me when he called. But it did disturb me that he knew her name. That's really why I called the police. How did he find out her name—and mine? He knew my first name. My name isn't listed in the book—just my husband George's."

Barbara then questioned her about any possible connection to the other women Dr. Sergeant had called. As expected, there was no relationship.

Barbara was close to leaving when Mrs. Herrera, who had been staring at a set of salt and pepper shakers on the table, looked up sharply.

She blinked, and looked at Barbara.

"You know," she said, "I was just thinking that I *did* give out some information about my family to someone I didn't know. It was a survey of some sort."

"When?"

Mrs. Herrera said that perhaps three or four months ago a man had called and said he was conducting a survey on household products and would she be willing to answer a few questions. "He said that I would be mailed some gifts for my trouble, and I said okay."

"What did he ask you?"

"A lot of questions about a wide variety of products, as I remember. All over the lot. About foods. Cleaning prod-

106

ucts. I've answered surveys like this before, and the questions are varied—they don't want you to know what they're really interested in."

"Did he ask you any personal questions?"

"That's my recollection, yes. He said I could choose not to answer them, but I remember he did ask me how many children I had and their names. Also my husband's name. And their ages."

"And you told him?"

"Yes."

"Did he identify himself?"

"He might have given me a name, but I don't remember what it was."

Barbara nodded. "Okay, I'm going to give you some tips on what to do in case this Dr. Sergeant calls back."

"I'd like that very much."

When Barbara got back to the station house, a new and depressing case had come in. A pregnant Hispanic woman had been killed by her boyfriend, but this had not prevented her from giving birth to a premature baby, who was alive and, seemingly, well.

But the mother, a junkie, had had AIDS, and it was likely that the newborn had AIDS too.

The people in Siberia, Barbara thought, were always inventing new ways to show you how inhuman they could be.

From her office, she called four other complainants. Three of the four remembered the survey, and they were glad to find out how Dr. Sergeant had found out about them.

She now knew where the guy was getting his information from. But she didn't know how he would be able to get an unlisted number to call.

And she didn't know why he had changed his pattern. For twenty years he had made thousands of calls to a wide variety of females. Then, over seven weeks, he called only women in their early fifties who had no discernible relationship to one another.

Why?

Barbara did not know. No matter how hard she tried, she couldn't get a handle on what bound these women together in his mind.

She was a bit worried.

What would he do next?

Chapter 28

Dr. Sergeant was sitting in his favorite armchair. He had his eyes closed, a smile on his face. He had a perfect picture of the scene.

He was in the back of a 1953 blue Chevrolet. He was sitting there with Audrey. The radio was on, and the only light was from a small yellow station bezel. "Pledging My Love" was playing.

The car was parked on a deserted street near Van Cortlandt Park, far off lovers' lane.

He could hear the voices.

"I'm a nice girl, Jackie. I've never done this with anyone before. I'm a little scared."

"You like me, don't you?" Dr. Sergeant—then Jackie—said, his throat thick with lust.

"Yes, I like you. But I'm afraid."

"Don't be afraid. Let me give you a little kiss."

"What if somebody comes by?"

"No one's going to come by."

Dr. Sergeant watched himself getting erect. He worked

109

at himself slowly, slowly with a Vaseline-slicked hand. He pictured his hands probing.

"Oh, Jackie. I've never been touched there before. Ohhh," Audrey said.

Dr. Sergeant pictured his hand snaking along the flat fourteen-year-old abdomen, then through the soft young pubic hair.

His finger found its place.

"Oh, Jackie. Oh Jackie. Oh Jackie."

Dr. Sergeant watched himself rising.

Part of him wanted to get it over with. Part of him couldn't stand it. But part of him wanted to make it last. And he could. He had experience. He had controlled himself thousands of times.

"Let me help."

She took her underwear off. Jackie was vaguely aware that the song was on the radio—"Pledging My Love."

Her underwear was off. He dropped his pants, then his underwear. He sprang free.

"Grab me," he said.

The edges of his mind were starting to float.

"Oh God," she said. "It's so big. Oh, it'll never fit."

Dr. Sergeant reached for the phone with the gloved hand. With the same hand he used a forefinger to dial the number, which he knew by heart.

"Hello?"

"Audrey?"

"Yes."

"Dr. Sergeant. I wanted to tell you that I'm not going to hurt you. I'll be gentle, I'll—"

There was a click.

Dr. Sergeant felt a surge of rage. He banged the phone down. It was only with great concentration that he was able to recreate the scene in the back of the Chevrolet so that it had a successful conclusion.

CHAPTER 29

On Friday, ten days before Christmas, Barbara got home at around midnight. Joe wasn't home. She knew how bad he wanted Toolan. She wouldn't be seeing a great deal of him.

She was feeling tired but pretty good. In the morning, she had testified at the trial of a gorilla pimp who had beaten one of his prostitutes with "pimp sticks"—wound-up wire hangers—so badly that she had almost died.

Barbara had worked on the case for months, had convinced the prostitute to testify, and the jury took exactly two hours before coming in with a guilty verdict.

So many times before, Barbara, and other cops, could see months and even years of work go down the drain because some slick lawyer was able to get a perp off. She was well aware that it was the system, and she believed in the system, but it was one of the ugliest feelings in the world, not only because a guilty person would walk free, but also because the same person would go right back to doing bad things.

But this guy wouldn't. The judge was Chester Knabb,

and there was no question that he had a dim view of pimps who brutalized the girls who worked for them. This pimp would be spending a long time upstate.

Deep down, it made Barbara feel very good. Cases like this made it all worthwhile. It kept her going.

She was in her kitchen, having a cup of tea, when the phone rang. That it was ringing this late didn't bother or alarm her in any way. Cops' phones rang at all kinds of odd hours.

"Hello."

"Detective Babalino?"

"Yes."

"This is Audrey Fontana."

"Hello. How are you?"

"I'm fine. I'm sorry to call you so late, but he . . . this Dr. Sergeant called again."

"What did he say?"

"Not much. I hung up on him."

"Do you remember what he did say?"

"He said, 'Hello, Audrey, I don't want to hurt you.' Then I hung up. Do you think he was threatening me?"

"No," Barbara said. "This isn't within the pattern of these people. They're not violent—except on the phone."

"Oh. I'm relieved to hear that."

"Good."

There was a pause.

"I did hear something else," Audrey said. "I mean besides what he said."

"What do you mean?"

"In the background. I heard music. There was music playing. A song I know—'Pledging My Love' by Johnny Ace."

"What's that?"

"Oh," Audrey said, "you're from a different generation. 'Pledging My Love' was a popular song back in the fifties. It was one of the first sort of rock-and-roll songs."

"Oh. Could you hold on a second?"

Barbara got off the phone and fished a pencil and notebook out of a nearby pantry drawer.

"Could you repeat the name of that song again?"

Audrey did.

"Thank you. I have a feeling he won't be calling you again."

They hung up.

Barbara finished her tea, thinking about the significance of the song. It was either a young perp who liked old songs, or an older guy whose music that was.

Somehow, Barbara felt she was getting closer to an answer.

CHAPTER 30

Lawless was well aware that they could not indefinitely keep up the surveillance on Charlie McCoy. Though Charlie was high most of the time, eventually someone was going to take a burn. Bad guys had a sixth sense, and would eventually spot a stakeout or tail. He was glad Francie and Jerry Collins were finally in a safe house.

They decided to make the collar on the fifth day after the surveillance began, and on the street. If he was a typical Bronxie, he would be well armed, and anyone breaking down his door would have problems.

They started their vigil at 6:00 A.M., waiting for McCoy to emerge from his building. The earliest he had come out during the previous five days was nine thirty, but you never knew.

In all, there were eight cops in on the collar: a couple at each end of the block, two on the roof, and two—Lawless and Gertz—in a car across the street.

At 10:00 A.M. McCoy emerged from his house.

He didn't look in the best of shape. His clothes were

rumpled, and he obviously hadn't shaved for a couple of days. There were dark marks under his light blue eyes, and the darkness acted as a kind of makeup that made them seem haunted.

As soon as he came out, the plan began.

Arnold Gertz emerged from the car.

For the occasion he was dressed in a red sweat suit. He wore his hair short; this plus his bulging muscles created the impression of an athlete (which, in fact, he was).

McCoy started to walk west on Bailey. Gertz quickly crossed the street and started walking behind him.

They walked up the block, Gertz closing ground with each step.

There was no one else on the street. Lawless was glad. If McCoy went for a piece, there could be gunfire.

When Gertz was within three yards of McCoy both McCoy and the detectives stiffened.

But one look convinced McCoy that Gertz was no threat.

Within the next six strides, McCoy suddenly found himself in the grasp of a human vise, and he was quickly aware that the street, empty two minutes earlier, was now alive with people running toward him.

"You're under arrest," Arnold said.

McCoy would have answered, but it's hard to talk when you're not breathing.

They interrogated McCoy in a room down at the Justice Department. Present were Mary Lee Baxter, Jim Ferguson, Delano Magee, and Lawless.

The questioning started at around 1:00 P.M.

The interrogation had a loose form.

First, they were going to talk with McCoy about his activities within the Bronxies.

This would then lead to a discussion of the homicide of Benny Ianello. They were going to try to get McCoy to talk more or less voluntarily and not threaten him with what they had until they had to.

When he didn't respond voluntarily, they started rolling out their weapons: Jerry Collins had flipped, and he had implicated both him and Toolan in the killing of Benny Ianello plus other people, as well as naming him as a drug dealer, an extortionist, and loan shark. It was hinted that if he cooperated, he could cut himself a deal.

McCoy did not respond to this. He just kept asking to call his lawyer.

After supper, the questioning got rougher.

The fact that they had recovered physical evidence on the Ianello homicide was brought in, and Lawless told McCoy that he knew exactly how it had happened.

This didn't have any effect either, so they played their ace card: they had put a wire on Francie Collins and had gotten McCoy's statements on tape that he had been involved in not only the Ianello killing but a number of others, as well as other racketeering activities for Toolan.

McCoy's response was simple: "Fuck you. I want to talk to my lawyer."

By 10:00 P.M. they decided to give up and let him call his lawyer. Lawless and the others were discouraged, but they didn't feel the ball game was over by any means. Witnesses would often stonewall interrogators on their initial contact. Later, as the trial drew near, or during the trial, or even after the trial when they were faced with substantial time, they would want to cut a deal.

Collins was held overnight for arraignment in the morning. He called his lawyer—a guy named Lee Jones, who often handled mobsters—who said he would be there.

The first step in trying to soften up McCoy was to get him into MCC awaiting trial with a high bail. This would depend to some degree on the judge. Federal judges were people first, and brought to the court various emotional baggage: some were soft, some were in the middle, a few were very tough.

116

The prosecutors were in luck. For the arraignment they got Judge Sean McCarthy, one of the toughest judges on the bench. The joke was that if you were a destitute mother who killed her husband because he abused their only child, McCarthy would have compassion—he would let the mother pick her form of execution.

McCoy's was the third case called.

Mary Lee Baxter made a strong case for no bail, emphasizing to the judge that McCoy was involved in at least four homicides and was part of the infamous Bronxies, which, like their Westies counterpart in Manhattan, were part of a conspiracy that had terrorized the Bronx for years.

Lee Jones argued vociferously that McCoy had not had any run-ins with the law for two years and that he had been gainfully employed (McCoy was listed on the books of a construction company owned by a cousin); that all in all he was a good citizen and that the charges were "baseless, without merit, the trumpeting of a prosecutor who somehow forgot what justice was."

Judge McCarthy allowed McCoy bail—of one million dollars.

Jones was furious, but Baxter was pretty happy, as were Lawless and the others. There was no way that McCoy was going to be able to raise $100,000 cash bond to cut himself loose, nor did he have anywhere near the property to get it from a bail bondsman. He was going to rot—and soften—in MCC.

CHAPTER 31

The safe house selected for the Collinses and their three kids was located just outside Laconia, a mid-sized town in central New Hampshire. It was owned by a friend and fellow prosecutor of Mary Lee Baxter's, a man named John Garth, who was a prosecutor in Boston. Garth, a bachelor, was in Palermo, and expected to be there for at least a month. The house would serve well until he came back.

At any rate, it was good to keep the subjects moving. If you stayed too long in one place word might find its way back to the wrong people.

The Collinses were safe. The only problem was boredom. It had started snowing in New Hampshire in October, and it snowed heavily through November. By the time the Collinses arrived at the house in mid-December there were ten inches of snow on the ground, and there was more to come. Temperatures rarely got above freezing and most of the time were well below. The weather was not conducive to going out.

Plus, even if they did get out—and each of them would

be able to, accompanied by three well-armed detectives—there wasn't much to do, particularly in winter unless you were a skier and ice skater, which neither Jerry nor Francie were.

They could stay and watch TV, but in New Hampshire the programming was much more limited than in New York. Francie didn't get all the game shows she usually watched.

Whatever, Jerry and Francie figured it beat dying.

CHAPTER 32

Lawless was in the squad room when he got the word. It was the day after Collins had been confined with a one-million-dollar bail in MCC.

Magee called him with disturbing news. "He's out, Joe. He got released this morning. Jones showed up with $100,000 in cash. There was nothing anybody could do about it."

"Where would he get that kind of money?"

"I don't know. The only one he knows is Toolan, and he's not tight with him anymore."

"How about the Family?"

"I don't think so. Since his star started to go down in Toolan's sky, the Mafiosi have started to avoid him. You know, their bread is buttered by Toolan."

It was a mystery.

"Did you get someone up to his apartment?"

"I got a couple of teams on it right now. But he was out a good half hour before I was informed. So if he's in the apartment, fine. They'll stay with him when he comes out

120

—though that will be hard because he'll likely suspect a tail. But if he's not there, I don't know where he is."

"Maybe it would be better to ring his bell," Lawless said. "If he's there, okay—if he's not, then we'll look for him."

There was a brief silence.

"Okay," Magee said. "Let's try it that way."

"How's Mary Lee reacting?" Lawless asked.

"She's pissed. She thought he deserved no bail. McCarthy will sometimes allow bail like this without rhyme or reason. This is the result."

"Okay," Lawless said, "I'll talk to you soon."

He hung up. Since awakening, he had had only one cigarette. Now totally unaware that he was doing so, he lit another.

He had been sitting at a desk. He got up and went over to the coffee urn. He poured himself a cup.

He tensed. This was not good.

Ten minutes later, his phone rang. He picked up. It was Magee.

"He's gone," Magee said. "They rang the bell, then had the super let them in. Nothing."

"Shit," Lawless said.

"Amen," Magee said. "I'll call Mary Lee."

"I'll get it on the wire."

Lawless tapped a cigarette from his pack. He used the butt of the cigarette he was smoking to light it.

CHAPTER 33

Charlie McCoy had tears in his eyes as he drove south along the New Jersey Turnpike.

In the end, Jimmy did care about him. It was the way it used to be when they were young.

Those were the fucking days. When the niggers and spics first started to come into the Bronx, and everyone started to run—run to somewhere else.

But Jimmy didn't run, and neither did Jerry, and neither did Charlie McCoy.

They formed their gang, the Bronxies, and the niggers quickly learned not to fuck with them.

Charlie smiled, remembering. They had this big gang, the Silver Spades, that thought they were going to drive this little gang of Irish kids out of the Bronx. So one night him, Jerry, and Jimmy kidnapped the big nigger homeboy who headed them Spades and took him out to the swamps of Jersey and took all his clothes off and then beat him to death with baseball bats.

Charlie remembered Jimmy smiling, his eyes glistening in the moonlight.

"Who says a Louisville slugger won't make a dent in the melon of a nigger?"

They had laughed their asses off at that one, and Jerry and him wanted to just leave the jig there, but Jimmy—Jimmy was always smart as a whip—he said no, that they got to send a message to them Spades.

"The message is they got to know who they're fucking with."

So they put the body in the trunk and drove back to the Bronx with it and dumped the carcass, nude, with a battered head with no features swollen three times normal, and they sent a message. Gradually the Spades came apart and the Bronxies owned most of the Bronx.

Charlie coughed slightly. Flanking him on the road were all the pipes and shit from the plants. Smelled like everybody in Jersey only shit here, nowhere else.

Charlie punched the lighter of the rented car, which he had borrowed from a wiseguy he knew, and lit a cigarette. He had no license—it had been suspended thirty-two times before he lost it—so he stayed within the speed limit.

Yeah, he thought, him and Jimmy were real close. Many a time they had been in the bars in the Bronx drinking, and those were happy times, scheming and planning and shit. Jerry was with them sometimes too.

Now, fucking Jerry. Jerry was a rat.

But not Charlie. Everybody thought the drugs had destroyed Charlie. But Charlie knew they hadn't. He had a little problem, but not so much that it could stop him. No fucking way.

Charlie was a little nervous about finding Jimmy's house. The fact was that he had never been invited there. The Diamond had bought the house for Jimmy years ago, and in all that time Jimmy had not invited Charlie.

They had had some bad arguments in the past two

years. He had told Jimmy that he was more beholden to the wiseguys than his old friends, and Jimmy said that wasn't true, that he was beholden to old friends that weren't junkies.

He was no fucking junkie! That was Jimmy's cunt of a wife talking. Veronica. What a cunt. An ugly cunt, too. She didn't care about nothing except bread. Friendship, that didn't matter a shit. She would suck off a greaseball with syph if it would turn a buck. She had been, was, and always would be a cunt.

Charlie took the exit Jimmy had told him to, and a short time later he was happy to see the name of he street: Mayo Place.

Down here in this town, Jimmy had said, all the street names were Irish; the Irish who had moved here from the various boroughs had the local government do it that way.

Jimmy's house was halfway down the block. It was a nice house, but nothing special. Charlie recognized Jimmy's Continental parked in the driveway, and Veronica's car parked on the street.

He pulled the car to a stop.

He took the .32 he had in his short coat and put it in his right pants pocket. You never knew about Jimmy. Charlie believed him to be sincere. But he had seen Jimmy when he was threatened. He could be slick.

Charlie got out of the car, carried his short coat over his shoulder, and went up the paved path to the front door.

It was open before he got there.

Jimmy Toolan was standing in it.

He was smiling. He always had a nice smile.

As he got closer, Charlie saw that Jimmy's blue eyes were twinkling, a little misty.

They embraced.

"Hey, Charlie," Jimmy said, "you stood up for me."

Charlie had tears in his eyes. So did Jimmy.

"Hey, Jimmy. We go back a long way. No fucking way is somebody going to flip me."

"I know," Jimmy said. "I know. Come on in."

Jimmy led him through the living room and into the kitchen. Veronica the cunt was at the stove stirring something.

"Hey, Veronica. Remember this guy?"

Veronica Toolan smiled. It occurred to Charlie that she had gotten fatter than ever. Jimmy probably had to derrick her onto his cock.

They embraced. She smelled of cooking grease.

"Hungry?" Veronica said.

"Thirsty," Charlie said.

She smiled. Jimmy laughed.

"White wine okay?"

"Super."

A half hour later, the three of them were in the dining room sipping wine. They were reminiscing about how Jimmy had learned how to dismember bodies while working in the butcher shop at Greenhaven kitchen.

Jimmy smiled. "It was the best thing I ever learned in the joint. Now you see 'em, now you don't."

They roared.

Charlie had been drinking his fair share of wine. So had Jimmy. So had Veronica.

Charlie felt some old feelings surging back.

"Hey, Jimmy," he said, "you're one fucking great guy. Everybody would have deserted me. Not you. You bet a hundred large on me. I can never forget that."

"Hey, buddy. No problem," Jimmy said. He reached across and touched Charlie's hand. "No way am I going to let Lawless and those other bastards put you down. I'm going to get you a top lawyer, and we're going to spread some bread around."

There was a silence while they drank.

"There is one favor you could do for me," Jimmy said.

"Name it."

"When I find Jerry and Francie, I want 'em gone. I need somebody I trust to do that for me."

"You're looking at him."

"All right," Jimmy said, "but don't just agree so quick. You're probably going to have to take out some cops to get the job done. There'll be mucho heat."

"I don't give a fuck. I'll do it."

"One other thing," Jimmy said, "and I don't want you to get pissed at me."

"What?"

"You got to be clean."

Charlie felt anger surge, but he controlled it. "Jimmy, I had a little problem. But no more. I'm clean."

Jimmy nodded.

Charlie was aware the cunt was watching him carefully. She was such a cunt.

They spent the rest of the afternoon watching a football game. Both Jimmy and Charlie fell asleep.

When they awakened, Charlie was set to drive back, but Jimmy wouldn't hear of it. "Stay the night," he said. "Go back fresh in the morning."

Charlie thought: Ho-ho, maybe I'll get to fuck Veronica. He was quite drunk.

He went to bed about eight o'clock, and so did Jimmy. They were both stewed.

Charlie awoke. He didn't know what time it was.

It was dark in the room, but the door was open. A little of the light from another room was coming in.

He turned around. There was a figure silhouetted.

"Jimmy?"

"Yeah. It's me."

Jimmy sounded strange, almost like he was crying or something. Charlie saw something that looked like a long stick in his hand. Adrenaline surged, clearing all cobwebs from Charlie's brain.

"Jimmy . . . Jesus . . ."

"You let yourself go, you dumb fuck. You let yourself go."

The .22 made a popping sound. One shot in the head was all that was needed. Jimmy had to jump back to avoid the spray of arterial blood.

CHAPTER 34

At around 10:00 A.M., the day after he was found dead in his bathroom by his girlfriend, Linda, Frank DeVito was autopsied in the Suffolk County morgue at Hauppauge, Long Island, by Fred Kaplan, an assistant M.E. In attendance from the city were George Benton and Vic Onairuts.

Pending results of toxicological tests, Kaplan fixed the cause of death as cardiac arrest.

"Disease?" Onairuts asked.

"He's got some deposits, but you know, I've seen the same in twenty-year-olds. Not enough to cause death."

Benton, avowed hypochondriac that he was, knew that atherosclerosis had indeed first been discovered in autopsies done on young American soldiers killed in Korea. Indeed, some guys in their twenties had deposits that one would expect to find in a man three times their ages. Gregory Peck's twenty-seven-year-old son, he remembered, was one such.

"So the scalding marks were incidental?" Onairuts said.

"Yes," Kaplan said, "all the evidence indicates he was standing when he was stricken. He has this big laceration on the back of his skull, and the detectives found blood on the edge of the toilet bowl—he hit his head when he fell, and then he just lay in that scalding water. He had to be there a couple of hours. I'm surprised he didn't lose more skin."

"Would you send me and George a copy of the protocol?"

"Sure. Got a card, George?"

"Sure."

"I guess that's it, Fred," Onairuts said. "Thanks."

"Anytime," Kaplan said. "Be well. Regards to the family."

Benton was glad when he exited the flat red brick building, one of a complex of low brick buildings that housed the Suffolk County Morgue. It was raining again and cold, and he could see the steam of his breath. He had a bizarre thought: proved he was living.

They had come out in Onairuts's car. They got in and started out down one of the roads that would lead them out.

"So what do you think, George?"

"I'm treating this and Rivera as homicides. No doubt now. There's no way that these are natural, wouldn't you say?"

"The odds against two guys in good shape like this, and their age, dying of a heart attack . . . you got a much better chance of winning the lottery."

"There's got to be a scam here somewhere."

"Inside."

"I'm working it like any homicide—from the inside out. See what's what. See if we can sniff out motive. Motive—that's the key here."

"Good luck."

"Thanks."

Onairuts turned his car onto a road that would lead them

to the Long Island Expressway, then to the Throgg's Neck Bridge and the Bronx.

On the way there was a delay because of an accident. Benton didn't notice anything. His mind was totally ab sorbed in the case.

CHAPTER 35

When he got back to the station, Benton made a call to a cop he knew in the Public Information Section of the Suffolk County P.D., John Jonas. He told Jonas that he wanted to get a look inside the DeVito house, and Jonas said he'd see what he could do.

A half hour later Jonas called back and told Benton that he could go out to the house anytime he wanted; that, in fact, the Suffolk County P.D. was through at the scene—it was no longer a police matter.

Benton called DeVito's house. Someone named Linda was there. He apologized for calling, explained who he was, and asked if he could come out and look. She said it would be all right.

They made an appointment to meet at three that afternoon.

Meanwhile, Benton had another place he wanted to look at again.

This time, Benton thought as he approached the municipal garage, his viewpoint was different. Last time it was because he had been instructed to investigate it. This time he was approaching it as a homicide. How or why, he didn't know—but there it was.

This time, too, he had some equipment together that would enable him to do a better job.

Willie, the attendant who had been on duty the night Rivera died, was in the kiosk. He recognized Benton.

Benton went up to the kiosk. Willie slid the window open.

"How you doing?" Benton said. "Remember me?"

"Yeah."

"Have you by any chance remembered anything else that might be helpful? Just anything at all?"

"No," Willie said. "What I says then is all I got."

"I see, thank you."

Benton looked toward where Rivera's Jaguar had been. There was a black BMW there.

"Would you mind," Benton said, "taking that BMW out of its space for a little while."

Willie nodded. "Okay."

Willie was briefly interrupted by a car coming in, but then he went back, backed the BMW out, and parked it in another slot not too far away.

Benton stood a few yards from the rear of the slot and slowly scanned the area.

The wall, except for an electrical receptacle which was almost out of sight at baseboard level behind the adjacent car, was a blank of concrete.

There was only a dim incandescent bulb lighting the scene.

Benton flicked on the battery-powered strobe light he had taken in.

He stepped closer to the slot and slowly played the light over the area, especially the floor. Maybe the killer had dropped something.

The floor was relatively clean for being the floor of a public garage, though there were, of course, assorted blotches and marks. There seemed, on closer examination now, to be a heavy collection of black powder on the driver's side, as if somebody had dumped out their ashtray, then spread it out.

Benton walked between the painted lines on the floor. There didn't seem to be anything else.

From a carrying case, he took out a small, powerful portable industrial vacuum.

He vacuumed the entire area in and around the slot, using separate bags for the black material and the rest of the floor.

When he was finished, he took a final look and started to walk, equipment in hand, to the second level.

It was not something another homicide detective would do. On the surface, it didn't make sense. Why walk to the top of a garage—Benton's intent—when the death had occurred on the first floor?

Partly, it was to get a better sense of the place—you could never tell when that would come in handy.

Secondly, just seeing all the cars parked, as Rivera's was, might make a connection for Benton that he would otherwise not see.

Occasionally, as he climbed, he had to stop to make way for cars passing by.

It took him about ten minutes to reach the top of the garage. He didn't think about having a coronary (except once)—a measure of his involvement in the case.

He took the elevator down, thanked Willie, and left.

He put the equipment in the trunk of his car and drove back to the NYPD crime lab downtown. He delivered the bags to John Williams, a bookish forensic technician who was one of the best in the business. Then he drove back to the station house.

CHAPTER 36

As he exited the expressway on his way to DeVito's house, Benton recalled that of all the people he had interrogated, DeVito had been surest that the witch doctor meant nothing.

And he had been the least afraid. Marcie Silverman, Rivera's secretary, had said that Rivera was definitely not afraid. Benton really wasn't all that sure how Gold felt. Herb Kellner was definitely afraid.

Yet you never really knew exactly what people were thinking. People were great actresses and actors. He knew he was. You went through your whole life pretending this, that, or the other thing.

Of course, when you were involved in a scam, then you made it a conscious point to act in a particular way.

Maybe one of these guys was acting. Maybe Kellner wasn't afraid. Maybe Gold wasn't what he seemed.

Maybe they were acting together.

Or maybe they weren't. Maybe whatever was going on was going on outside their control.

Benton found DeVito's house without any problem.

It reminded him of DeVito: a big, brash place, with massive columns—obvious phallic symbols—in front.

Two cars were parked in the turnaround: a white Eldorado and a red Volvo.

Benton parked in a corner of the turnaround and went up to the door. He had with him the strobe, the vacuum, and fresh bags.

He pressed the bell and heard it chime inside.

The woman who opened the door was pretty in a hard-edged, glossy kind of way but suffered from using too much makeup. Her eyelids were empurpled, the lid edges lined with black, her face was rouged, her eyebrows tweezed, her lips were heavy with lipstick, her hair was frizzy and cold, too young for the lines on her face. Faintly, under her eyes, there were smudge marks. She had probably been crying.

"I'm George Benton," he said.

"Yeah, come in."

"I appreciate you allowing me to take a look here," Benton said.

"Well, if anyone did this to Frank, I want to know."

Benton nodded. "Are you up to telling me what happened?"

Linda proceeded to recount how she had come in and first noticed it was so damp, then had seen the water on the floor and had gone up and discovered him. As she did, she more or less walked through it—but she declined to go into the bathroom.

"It was horrible," she said.

Benton nodded. Part of him watched her closely. "Do you know where he was before he came home?"

"No."

"Thank you," he said.

For a while, Benton examined the stairs and the area at the base of the stairs. Then he climbed the stairs to the bathroom.

The door was partially open. He pushed it all the way open.

The room was neat, clean, as if someone had cleaned up. There was no blood on the toilet bowl where he had hit his head.

Terrific. Shit.

Benton stepped inside. The bathroom was large and overdone, like the rest of the house.

The sink and toilet were made of gray marble; the faucet handles were immense gold fish.

In truth, there was not much to examine.

But he did.

Over the next hour he disassembled the sink trap, storing the material from it in a plastic pouch, then used a wire hook to scoop as much material as he could from the shower trap.

Then he vacuumed the rug and, finally, used the strobe to carefully examine the entire bathroom. He also examined the contents of the medicine chest. Nothing remarkable.

He thanked the woman and then left.

He took the expressway back. As he did, he reflected that perhaps some important evidence had been washed away by the cleaning lady. Like fingerprints.

He would have to go with what he had, and hope that something was there.

CHAPTER 37

Charlie McCoy was found on 191st Street and 192nd Street—the body on 191st, the head on 192nd, in St. James Park.

He was found by a reporter for the *New York Post*, who had received an anonymous telephone tip on where to find his remains. The reporter, whose name was Donna Kennedy, was extremely upset, but she was back at her terminal by midnight, batting out an exclusive story.

As he looked at the torso at the scene, nothing showed on Lawless's face. But inside he burned. This was Toolan's work. He was sending a message, a message of ferocity. He would stop at nothing—including whacking out a guy he had known since he was a little kid—when his survival was threatened.

And Toolan had made sure, Lawless thought, that he got his one hundred large back by producing McCoy's body. It all worked out so neatly.

* * *

During the day, Lawless dropped in to a couple of bars where lower-echelon Bronxies congregated. The mood was plain: fear. They didn't want to talk with Lawless; they didn't even want to be seen with him.

Later, Magee, Baxter, and Lawless held a meeting downtown in Baxter's office. They discussed whether to try to collar other members of the Bronxie crew who had been named by Collins and McCoy, or to wait.

They unanimously agreed to wait. There was simply too much fear now. They had pretty good stuff against the gang members to make them start flipping, but they decided to wait a couple of weeks until the fear abated.

Even if it all went bad—if they weren't able to turn anyone else—they still had Jerry and Francie Collins plus McCoy's taped statements and the physical evidence of the Ianello homicide. Baxter figured she could go to trial right now and have a good chance of convicting Toolan and other Bronxies on multiple RICO charges. But she, Magee, and Lawless wanted to get enough to make it a sure thing.

Lawless needed no reminders, though, to know that now Toolan was going to make an all-out effort to find and whack the Collinses. They were all that stood between him and freedom.

Lawless knew that he and his team were going to have to be extremely vigilant.

CHAPTER 38

Jimmy Toolan sat opposite Johnny Pergola. They were in a booth by a picture window in a diner on the Jersey Turnpike. It was morning. A light snow was falling. It was the day after McCoy's body had been discovered.

Toolan and Pergola were physical opposites.

Toolan was blond, blue-eyed, smooth, almost baby-faced, and tended toward chunkiness; Pergola was thin, with black hair and dark eyes and skin that had suffered five years of teen acne.

"So how's Veronica and the kids?" Pergola said, lighting an unfiltered Camel.

"Good. She's good. The kids are doing fine down here. Better than in the city, with all those spics and niggers."

"Yeah," Pergola said, "that's why I moved out of the city. Those fucking colored animals! They should send 'em all back to fucking Africa."

"Yeah," Jimmy said. He scooped up some scrambled eggs with his fork and chewed slowly.

The preliminary bullshit, both men knew, had been completed.

"So how can we help you, Jimmy?"

Jimmy said nothing. The silences in his conversation tended to grip one's attention, because you didn't know what he was going to say next—and because it was Jimmy Toolan.

Jimmy smiled. "You're not wearing a wire, are you?"

"What are you fucking kidding?" Pergola said. Anybody else he might have slapped in the noggin.

"Of course," Jimmy said.

There was an uncomfortable silence, then Jimmy spoke. "You know the problem, right?"

"You mean with the Collinses?"

"Yeah. I'd like them out of my life."

"We'll do the best we can."

"I'm willing to pay a half million dollars for both of them. Individually, three fifty large for Jerry, one fifty large for Francie. Got that?"

"Yeah. You'll have everybody and his fucking mother looking for that."

"That's the idea," Jimmy Toolan said and continued eating his breakfast.

CHAPTER 39

Barbara Babalino was out in the field most of the time, but when she got back to the station house there were two messages waiting for her. One was from Mrs. Herrera, the lady from Mineola.

She called her. Mrs. Herrera picked up on the first ring.

"He called again," she said. "About a half hour ago."

"What did you do?" Barbara asked.

"I didn't do anything for ten seconds. He was trying to engage me in conversation, but I didn't respond. Then I just hung up."

"Good."

"It was different this time, though."

"What do you mean?"

"I heard music in the background."

"What?"

"It was very clear. I recognized the song. From the fifties. Rosemary Clooney singing "C'mona My House.""

"A fifties star?"

"God, she was one of the biggest singing stars when I was young."

"No other significance?"

"No. Just a song from schooldays."

"Okay," Barbara said. "Thanks very much for calling."

"Do you think he'll call again?"

"I doubt it."

They hung up.

The door to Barbara's office had been open. She got up and closed it, then made a fresh pot of coffee and sat down to think about the case.

There was no question, she thought, that this Dr. Sergeant wanted his victims to hear the music. Why? And why the music from the fifties? What significance did that have to Dr. Sergeant?

Barbara did not know. She sipped the coffee.

Somehow, she thought, if he called one of these middle-aged women again, she was sure the woman would also be treated to the background music of the fifties.

That was an added part of his routine.

That was . . .

Barbara froze for a moment. She put the coffee cup on her desk.

She had an idea. It was very simple, but she had to test it.

She called Mrs. Herrera back because Barbara figured she would be in.

"Hello." The voice was edged with trepidation.

"It's just Detective Babalino," Barbara said. "I was wondering. What's your maiden name?"

"Carter."

"Oh."

"Why?"

"I have an idea. I'll get back to you."

Over the next half hour, Barbara made four additional

calls, all to the middle-aged complainants. Three of the four were in.

Barbara asked them two questions: What was their maiden name? Did they know any of the other victims by their maiden names?

They did.

They all knew each other—from grammar school!

Then she called each back and asked two other questions: Could they think of anyone they knew from those days who might do something like this?

None did.

And: How would this Dr. Sergeant get their telephone numbers if he only knew their maiden names?

Mrs. Fontana, the first complainant, provided an answer. "From the reunion."

"What's that?"

"Our grammar school, Our Lady of Refuge, last year celebrated its sixty-fifth anniversary. A lot of us were there. They had a program with the names, addresses, and telephone numbers of people who wanted to make further contact with other people. It was quite an affair."

Jesus, Barbara thought. That's where the basic information comes from.

But who was he? And why was he doing this?

And why to these particular ex-students? Was there anything special about them?

CHAPTER 40

Barbara took the IND subway a few stops to the 196th Street Station, then walked down a couple of blocks to Our Lady of Refuge.

The school was in northern Siberia, five or six blocks above Fordham Road at Briggs and 196th Street, and adjacent to Public School 46. There was a church attached to the school.

Barbara knew the area well. The P.S. 46 schoolyard, a vast asphalt area next to the school and enclosed by a Cyclone fence, was a popular area for neighborhood drug dealers.

Like the rest of Siberia, the area was run-down, and the school and even the church itself had graffiti scrawled on them. Barbara assumed that some of the people who had attended the school's reunion had visited the school again. It must have been a bittersweet experience.

At the lobby level there was a security guard who stopped her. She showed her shield, then climbed one long flight of stairs to the first floor, where the administrative offices were.

A few minutes later she was sitting in the office of the principal, Sister Marie Anne, a woman in her early forties who wore lay clothing.

Barbara had called ahead, so the principal knew what she wanted. She took a manila envelope off her desk and handed it to Barbara. "Here is the list of all the alumni who paid their thirty-five dollars and, we assume, came to the reunion. I've also enclosed a program that lists the current addresses and telephone numbers of these people."

Barbara had taken the material out and was looking at it.

"The year they graduated, see, is shown here," the principal said.

Barbara looked. The columns of names were broken up by year, starting back in the thirties.

Under 1951 there were maybe twenty-five names, maybe fifteen males and ten females. From 1952 there were twenty-two names, twelve of whom were female.

Barbara grew excited when she saw that seven of the names of the females who had gone to the reunion had maiden names she already knew. There were four from 1951 and three from 1952.

And maybe, among the male names, was the name of the perp.

"Did anyone come to the school," Barbara said, "asking for this list?"

"Not that I know of."

She pressed the intercom. The Spanish receptionist, a young woman, appeared in the doorway.

"Alice, do you know if anyone requested to see this list since it was published?"

"Not that I know of."

"Thank you," Sister Marie Anne said, and turned to Barbara. "I guess not."

Which meant, Barbara thought, that only people who

attended the reunion would know the numbers of the women who were called, except for the principal, secretary, people involved in printing the booklet, and perhaps some others who had had incidental contact with it that Barbara didn't know about.

"Thank you very much, sister," Barbara said, "if you have any ideas about who might be doing this, please call."

"I will," Sister Marie Anne said.

CHAPTER 41

Barbara took the material back to the apartment to study. She made herself a cup of coffee, then sat down with it at the kitchen table.

Most of the people on the list lived in the suburbs, Nassau, Suffolk, White Plains, Jersey. Eight—five females and three males—lived in the city: three in the Bronx, three in Queens, and two in Manhattan.

Just looking at the list, there was nothing unusual. Just ordinary names, names of kids who had gone to a parochial school in the Bronx. Irish names, Italian names, others.

She realized, as she perused the list, that it was entirely possible that the perp was not on it. There could have been somebody who simply had gotten hold of the list.

Maybe, but Barbara doubted it. She figured that the person who was harassing these women knew them from way back when. That he had gone to Our Lady of Refuge, too.

She sipped her tea and then a gradual realization came to her.

There were twenty-two women on the list. He had focused on five. Why? Why these and not others?

Maybe these were the only ones he could contact. Maybe . . .

Barbara leafed through the case folder and from it she extracted the list of complainants. She would try to see. She picked up the phone.

Mrs. Herrera, née Carter, answered.

"Hi, Mrs. Herrera, Barbara Babalino. How are you?"

"Better. I'm starting not to worry about being called, thank God."

"Good. I went to Our Lady of Refuge and got a list of the people who were at the reunion. I was trying to determine if any of the people that you knew had something in common back then. I mean, did you belong to a special club, or live close to one another . . . I don't know."

Mrs. Herrera answered immediately. "We were all cheerleaders."

"Really?"

"Sure. We had a very good basketball team then, even though we were a small school, and the principal went all out. Being a cheerleader was a big deal then, too. Girls competed pretty hard for the spots."

Barbara had nothing to say. She didn't know where to take it. Then: "were you ever harassed in any way when you were young?"

"No," Herrera said, "no more than anyone else. Not like this."

"Okay," Barbara said. "Thanks."

After she hung up, Barbara called Mrs. Fontana.

She also said that she had been a cheerleader. Beyond that, there was nothing.

Essentially, Barbara was at a dead end. Assuming that the perp was on the list, there was no way that Bledsoe would allow her to launch an investigation into each of the people.

She was going to have to come up with something else.

She was pretty sure that Dr. Sergeant was going to call back one of the remaining women on the list.

Maybe she could get phone traps—devices the phone company could place that record incoming callers' numbers—installed, but she wondered if she could show a judge enough so he'd authorize them.

And what if he did and her theory was wrong? What if those remaining women weren't called?

She got up and got herself a cup of coffee and sat back down.

She sipped the coffee.

Then she had an idea. It would involve calling all the men on the list, and, though it might seem like the longest road to the perp, it might actually be the shortest.

CHAPTER 42

Four days after he gave them the tracings from DeVito's bathroom and the garage floor, Benton checked with forensic. Like everyone at this time of year they were jammed up and would not have anything to report for a couple more days.

Benton thanked them and hung up.

For a moment his mind strayed, and he thought of his daughter. He was starting to doubt if she was going to write. Or at least send a card. It was almost Christmas.

He tried to refocus on the case without much success. Then he relaxed, let his thoughts wander, take him wherever they were going to go.

They were not too far, he thought, from deep winter. He hated the winter. Most people didn't realize it, but the winter was a very lonely time. As a kid, he had spent a lot of time alone in his house in downtown Manhattan when his mother and father were at work, and he used to sit by the window and look down into the street. Many times kids would gather to play stickball, or in the fall touch football, and he used to watch the game.

He got to feeling that he was part of the game, even though he wasn't athletic—he never believed in himself as an athlete too much.

But in the winter the streets were cold and empty, so incredibly cold and empty, and he used to feel so terribly alone that sometimes he would just start to cry.

He never told anyone about his loneliness because, as he and Dr. Stern later discussed, he didn't believe that anyone would care. More, they would view it as a burden.

But it was one thing to discuss it, another to make the bad feelings go away. That took so long, because they had been a long time building.

He had an insight. Over the winter he knew he would be lonely, but if he had a card from Beth, to some degree he wouldn't be, because it wasn't really the card that he would have, but Beth's love.

And other cops. That was important. That was a fraternity that he sometimes felt so alien to but so much a part of. There was love there, too.

He smiled. But the problem sometimes was not the absence of love, but that the receiver couldn't feel it deep enough for it to make a difference. It was a leaf against a tide of noncaring.

Still, deep down he believed in the power of love.

His mind clicked. He thought of Herb Kellner.

Benton could understand Kellner very well. He was the kind of guy who was always afraid—like him. Something like this would freak him out.

Never mind having other suspicions. Even if he wanted to, Kellner couldn't fool Benton. They were comrades in arms.

Which focused him on David Gold. Mr. Oil.

Burke had sent over the D&Bs on the partners in Parcel 19, plus the reports of Kellner's company and Wishbone, Gold's company, having gone public.

He read all the material about the officers of both corporations.

They seemed to have all the proper credentials.

He got up and went to the window and looked out.

Parcel 19 had to be the answer.

Was it going to be developed in some way? It would seem that the partners in it would have gotten wind of that.

Maybe one knew that it was going to be big and was killing all the others. If that was so, why go to such elaborate lengths? Just kill them all at once.

Weird.

Benton realized that he just didn't know what the details of the agreement among the partners were. Maybe if he understood that, he could come to some conclusions.

But it all started and ended with Parcel 19. He had to find out what its significance was in this whole thing, if any. Then, maybe, he could work from there.

CHAPTER 43

Benton had to make a couple of calls to contacts in city government before he was able to determine which city department would be able to indicate what was special, if anything, about Parcel 19.

In all, getting to the right person took about three hours —something of a bureaucratic miracle—and at around 2:00 P.M. he was in an elevator on his way up to see John Vickers, director of the CDC—the City Development Corporation.

Benton only had to wait a few minutes before he was led across a bullpen of desks at which sat men and women, most in front of computers. The place had a bureaucratic feel to it. The joke was that the paint—usually green or blue—used to paint city offices was manufactured in asylums by people suffering from depression.

Vickers' office was, by contrast, bright and cheerful. It had a wood rather than a metal desk, a carpet, and windows that had a spectacular view of Lower Manhattan.

Vickers was himself very unbureaucratic. He was about

forty. He was well dressed and had his hair styled. He was more yuppieish than one usually found in city government, but Benton didn't sense the narcissism one associates with yuppies.

Benton showed his shield, and Vickers directed him to a leather seat in front of the desk. "How can I help you, sir?"

"Well," Benton said, "before I tell you what I need, I was wondering if it could be just between you and me. It's rather delicate."

Vickers got up from his desk and went around it to the door, which was open. He closed it and went back to his desk. "No problem."

"We have been conducting an investigation into the death of Charles Perez, holder of a parcel of land in the Bronx, and my investigation has led me to believe that the death—which doesn't look like a homicide, but I think is—is linked to that land. I understand that your department might have information on what, if anything, is going to happen to it. On the surface it doesn't seem to have value. But we ask ourselves: Why are people— and there's another death involved—who are linked to this parcel of land dying?"

"What's the parcel?"

"It's called Parcel 19."

Vickers, Benton thought, was good. But down through the years he had interrogated thousands of suspects and perps, and he could read reactions—except when he was at war with the demons inside himself—extremely well. Vickers, as they say, had blinked, despite himself. He had suppressed his reaction.

"Parcel 19," he said. "I don't have any particular insight into this. I'm not that familiar with it. If something was going to happen to it, I would know."

Benton looked at him. Benton knew. This guy was lying. Maybe he had something to do with the whole thing.

Benton had a variety of ways to go, one of which was to get up and walk out the door. But sometimes he could be, crazily, a bulldog. Now was one of those times.

"I understand your reluctance," Benton said, "to say anything about the parcel. But I must also say this. If there is anything to be said about it, please do so. There could be additional homicides connected with it."

Vickers looked at him. Vickers had not denied anything. Benton knew for sure that his instinct was correct. Vickers knew something about Parcel 19 that Benton should know.

Vickers was perturbed. He stood up. "The thing that bothers me," he said, "is that someone in this office must have leaked information—assuming what you say is correct."

"What is it?"

Vickers looked at Benton. "And now," he said, "I must ask you to promise not to reveal anything about our conversation to anyone."

"You have my word."

"In about one month, Parcel 19 is going to be worth its weight in gold. A month ago it was selected by our executive committee as the site of a new complex of hospital facilities in the Bronx. This is a $500 million project, and that land is going to be worth at least . . . you can imagine . . . to the owners."

Benton was excited. He had the beginning of an answer, the beginning of a motive.

"But you don't own it. How can you be sure it will be sold to you—I mean theoretically?"

"We have a buy-back clause. But we'd have to pay fair market value based on estimates of final real estate value. In other words, once the project is complete, its value on that year's real estate market is calculated and the money paid according to the top estimate. The owners are in an incredibly good position—they paid only a half million for it."

"Who's the executive committee?"

"Seven people, all city employees who consider all such projects."

"Could one of them have leaked the information?"

"Yes. But none of them could benefit, unless they knew someone, say, who had an opportunity to buy it. Actually, it's a fait accompli for us. We don't care who owns the parcel. We have our option to buy, and we're going to."

"What you're saying is that if someone had this inside information they might try to buy it from the partners."

"That's right. That's one possibility."

Benton nodded. "I guess that's about it," he said. "I very much appreciate your being candid with me."

"That's okay," Vickers said, "but I would appreciate it, if you find that someone from here is involved in a leak, that you tell me before any media person."

"I don't speak to the media," Benton said.

He stood up, and Vickers led him out. As he passed through the bullpen, he realized that any one of the twenty to thirty people here might have leaked the information.

At the elevator, he shook hands with Vickers, then left. But he was distracted because something had occurred to him.

Back at the station, he read the report. It was just a detail in a lot of details that had been provided on the individual by the New York Exchange. It said: "former consultant to CDC." It was four words, but it told Benton what path he should take. He no longer needed instinct to guide him on who might be bad. The citation was part of the bio on David Gold, Mr. Oil.

156

CHAPTER 44

Happily, unlike Kellner, his secretary was not the panicky type. Benton asked for the number and address where Kellner was staying, and she gave it to him readily.

"Who else knows his whereabouts?" Benton asked.

"Just me, you, and Mr. Gold."

Benton nodded. Something shifted in his stomach. "Could I use the phone here?"

"If you want privacy," the secretary said, "you can use Mr. Kellner's office."

"Thank you."

Kellner picked up on the first ring.

"Mr. Kellner, George Benton. How are you?"

"I feel better here than in the city."

"Good. I think I've been able to figure out a few things."

"Really?"

"Yes. Can you answer a couple of questions?"

"Sure."

"What exactly is the nature of your contractual agree-

157

ment with Rivera, DeVito, and Gold on Parcel 19?"

"Four-way split. We each put in a quarter of the money to buy it. If we resell, we each get a quarter of the profits."

"What happens if partners die, as they have?"

"The surviving partners have the option to buy within sixty days of the death of the particular partner."

"I see," Benton said, and he surely did. Though it still didn't make complete sense.

"I'll tell you what," Benton said, "until this thing is resolved, why don't you go somewhere else—and don't tell *anyone* where you've gone. I'll give you my number so you can contact me once you get settled."

"No one?"

"No one at all. Not even your secretary."

"Christ, you're scaring me."

"I don't mean to. I just want to make sure you're okay. And you will be if you do what I suggest."

"When?"

"As soon as possible. Today."

CHAPTER 45

Two weeks after Jimmy Toolan and Johnny Pergola met in the diner on the New Jersey Turnpike they met again.

They sat at the same table, both drinking black coffee.

"We got a hundred fucking button men beating the bushes for these fuckers—nothing. They're buried in ice," Pergola said. "We were thinking that maybe we could try to follow one of the cops to wherever they are. Lawless is the guy."

Toolan shook his head. "No, he's much too smart. Whoever follows him will end up on the wrong end."

"All we can do is keep looking."

"I'm going to raise the ante," Jimmy said.

Pergola looked at him.

"Another 250 large for both of them."

"I don't know if bread alone is going to do it, Jimmy."

"It can't hurt," Jimmy said.

* * *

At home, Veronica Toolan was just placing a sandwich in front of her son, Brian, a red-haired freckle-faced sixteen-year-old.

The boy dug into the sandwich; as he did he read a magazine.

Jimmy Toolan loomed in the doorway. There was a momentary hitch in the boy's eating, but you wouldn't notice unless you knew him quite well. Then he resumed at his regular pace. He didn't look up.

Toolan signaled with his eyes for his wife to come out of the kitchen. She did. She followed Toolan down the hall to the master bedroom. They went inside and she closed the door behind them.

Toolan turned. "The wiseguys can't find them," Toolan said.

"We got to find them, Jimmy. Somehow. Those fucks'll take us all down. They probably could indict on what they got."

There was silence. They had discussed more than once how they could find the Collinses. There was no fresh ground to plow.

"All the times I spoke with that little cunt," Veronica said, referring to Francie Collins. "I wish I could remember something we could use."

"Where's her mother?"

"Who knows?"

"Father?"

"He died years ago. Only a few years ago they found he had been buried in Potter's Field. They left him there."

"I was thinking about Jerry," Toolan said. "I can't think of no close relations that we could use. His parents are dead. One brother he had I know died in a heist. His one sister I think she was out west somewhere."

"I was just thinking," Veronica said, "that Francie once mentioned to me where her mother lived. I just remembered—I think."

"Where?"

"Kings Park." Veronica paused. "On Long Island. Yeah."

"She alive?" Jimmy said. His interest had increased.

"I don't know. This is something Francie told me a couple of years ago. She should be. Francie ain't that old."

"Why don't we try it?"

"I don't know what name she's under. I don't know Francie's maiden name. Her mother was Mary, I think."

"I do," Jimmy said. "Jerry told me once. I remember he said it was Muldoon, rhymed with moon."

"Let's go."

When they got to the kitchen the boy was gone.

To try to make contact with Francie's mother, Toolan and his wife traveled a good three miles from their own house to make the call. They assumed, always, that their own phones were bugged, and they also assumed that local phones within a radius of a mile of their house were also tapped. Many a wiseguy had gone away because he thought that just because phones were public they were clean.

Veronica did the calling.

First, she called information.

A Mary Muldoon was listed. And, unlike in Jersey, the address was given by the operator on request: 23 Marvin Drive.

She dialed the number, and they dropped $2.50 in change into the phone.

The phone rang three times.

"Hello?" An older voice.

"Yes, is Mary Muldoon there?"

"This is Mary. Who's this?"

"I was wondering if you'd be interested in buying some magazines."

The phone went dead. Jimmy and Veronica hugged each other.

CHAPTER 46

Barbara was in her office. She had a jack attached to the phone and the other end plugged into a tape recorder. So far she had made twenty calls to the men on the Our Lady of Refuge list. Over a two-day period she had succeeded in reaching fourteen of them.

Barbara had made a little chart which included the name of the person called and the time. Of the fourteen people contacted, most had been contacted after six. Two had been contacted during the day—one, John Lock, at around three o'clock, and another, Raymond O'Malley, at ten in the morning.

Barbara's procedure had not been by any means scientific.

She had called all of the numbers during the day. If a woman answered she would ask for the man. If the person said the person wasn't in she'd say she'd call back, then she'd call back at night and ask for them.

If she got them, the rap would be the same.

Now she took a little breath and dialed the next number.

It occurred to her that she was really starting to polish her presentation.

"Hello," a male voice answered.

"Mr. Geehan?"

"Yes."

"My name is Barbara Babalino. I'm working with Our Lady of Refuge, helping them organize a communion breakfast next April. I was wondering if you would be interested in attending."

"Sure. I'd like to go."

"Fine. Let me send you some literature on it."

"Good. You do that."

Now, Barbara thought, she had fifteen voices on tape. It had taken two days. Just that morning Bledsoe had called her into his office and asked her what kind of progress she was making. She had told him a lot. He wasn't impressed. Progress to him was the perp on videotape with a smoking gun. She figured she was going to have to close ground on this guy quickly.

She decided to go with what she had now. She would play the tapes to the victims, independently, and see if they could recognize the voice.

She started to call them to make appointments to play the tape.

By four the next afternoon Barbara was on her way to Mrs. Herrera's house in Mineola.

In her pocketbook were the recorder and tape.

She had already played the tape to three of the complainants.

Barbara was excited. Two of the three had identified the voice of one of the people she had called as Dr. Sergeant.

His name was John Lock.

Barbara figured to play the tape one more time. If she got a positive voice ID one more time she would make some moves toward collaring the guy.

The strange thing about the ID was that the women

didn't really remember exactly who this John Lock was. Admittedly, it was a long time ago—thirty-six or thirty-seven years—but he was just a name. None of them knew him personally, one sort of remembered him as being small, cute in a mousy kind of way, and quiet.

Barbara thought that that was consistent with the kind of profile obscene telephone callers had: they usually stayed in the background; they were rarely outgoing personalities.

Mrs. Herrera met her at the door. There was a man behind her. Mrs. Herrera introduced him as her husband, George.

Barbara did not set up the recorder right away. The idea in any identification, just as it was in an interrogation, was to relax the person as much as possible. Make it seem as far removed from a police situation as possible. People did much better when they were relaxed.

Barbara set the recorder up on the kitchen table and started the tape. Both Mrs. Herrera and her husband listened.

Sergeant was the fourth person she had called.

Barbara made no sign that Sergeant was the voice the other women had identified.

Half the conversation had been completed when Mrs. Herrera said: "Wait. That's him. That's this Dr. Sergeant!"

Barbara turned off the tape. She nodded.

"Okay, let's listen to the rest of it."

She turned the recorder back on. Mrs. Herrera listened to the rest of it. As she did she nodded—this was definitely the man.

Barbara turned off the recorder. "His name is John Lock. Do you remember him?"

Mrs. Herrera tried to remember. "I remember the name, but I don't remember him too well. He was small, I think. Then again, most of us weren't too huge back in the eighth grade."

She paused.

"If he's the person, why do you think he's doing it?"

"I don't know," Barbara said. "He's probably got his own reason—a disturbed one. I'm not sure."

There was silence.

Mr. Herrera attracted Barbara's attention. He was laughing.

"I wonder if he was making a joke," Mr. Herrera said.

"What do you mean?" Barbara said.

"Well, I'm in the hardware business. His name is Lock, and Sergeant is the name of a high-quality line of locks."

Barbara half smiled. "Really?"

"That's right."

"I wouldn't have known."

"Maybe that's why he picked it," Mr. Herrera said. "You would have known if he called himself Segal or Yale, right?"

"Maybe . . . and maybe he's using the name because he wants to get as close to being known as possible—without being known."

Before she left, Barbara asked Mrs. Herrera if she'd be willing to testify against Lock if he were indicted.

She said that she would.

There were still four women Lock hadn't called. Barbara figured that he would—for sure. All she had to do was get approval to install phone traps. Dr. Sergeant would soon be making his calls from the dayroom of some prison.

CHAPTER 47

Once he had focused on Gold, Benton pulled out all the stops. He checked his yellow sheet, DMV, and probed state and federal tax returns—usually confidential—through his contacts.

He was surprised. Except for a few parking tickets, there was no negative information on Gold.

He made another goosing-type call to the forensics lab about mid-morning on the sixth day since he had delivered the tracings to them.

There was nothing extraordinary in the reports. The tracings consisted of material that one might expect on the floor of a garage—oil, asbestos, etc. The powdery material that Benton picked up from the floor on the driver's side was carbon. Benton assumed this was also a vehicular product.

The materials vacuumed from the floor and drains of DeVito's house were also routine—hair, soap, various shreds of wrappers. The only unusual item was minute traces of salt.

What, Benton thought, was salt doing on the floor of a bathroom?

Maybe the guy ate something there?

It seemed unlikely.

Benton spent at least fifteen minutes poring over each of the reports.

He had nothing, except there was one little detail that couldn't be explained: the salt. Why?

He called the lab and got John Williams on the phone.

"John, George Benton."

"How you doin'?"

"John, this report on the bath that was sent to me. Everything makes sense except the salt. I can't explain why that's there. Can you?"

"No. Unless somebody was eating something salty in there."

"Do people bathe with salt water?"

Williams chuckled. "You know how people are—never know what they're going to do."

"Let me ask you this: Can you think of any other use for salt other than on food?"

"Salt alone, no? Salt water is used as a conductor. It enhances electrical conductivity. They moisten the pads on electrical contacts for the electric chair with salt water."

"Really?" Benton said softly. Jesus.

"Yeah," Williams said, and then went into a dissertation on the electromechanical properties of salt. But Benton wasn't listening.

"What about carbon?" Benton asked, holding his breath.

"An excellent conductor too. You know, that's why they use carbon in batteries."

"Jesus Christ," Benton said. "Thanks."

Onairuts wasn't in when Benton called, but his assistant said he was due back in twenty minutes. Did Benton want to call back?

"I'm coming down," he said. "Please tell him to wait for me. It's very important."

"Sure."

As it happened, Benton was entering Bellevue, site of the M.E.'s office, just as Onairuts was arriving.

They stood in the hall and talked.

"We found salt on the floor of DeVito's bath. We found carbon on the floor of the garage right where Rivera stood. Christ, could they have been electrocuted? I thought you had to have a lot more than household current to get killed."

"Not really," Onairuts said. "You can be killed with anything from fifty volts up. The idea is that if you get enough voltage passing through you the heart goes into arrest, but there wouldn't be characteristic scorch marks and trauma associated with electrocution."

"Jesus. That's what they did here! They somehow got wires from electrical sources and—"

Onairuts chimed in. "DeVito and Rivera were well grounded, DeVito with salt water, Rivera's feet in carbon. They took just enough of a shock to stop heart action—and not leave any traces."

"But where's the wire?" Benton said. "We found nothing."

"That I couldn't tell you."

But there was someone who could.

Benton called Williams from one of the lobby phones in Bellevue.

He set up the scenario with Rivera and DeVito, and Williams had an explanation for no wire.

"What could have been done is that someone strung a really thin-gauge wire from an outlet to the car. When Rivera touched the car, which was all hot, he became part of the circuit. The wire could have been made thin enough so that while it could pass the current, it vaporized as it did because it was so thin. We did find trace elements of copper, you know, in both places."

"Christ, how malevolent," Benton said. "And they probably hooked up a wire to a faucet or something in the bath. DeVito, standing in salt water, touched the faucet and was belted by enough voltage to stop his heart."

"You got it," Williams said.

"Malevolent," Benton said.

CHAPTER 48

A half hour after he spoke with Williams, Benton was walking into the municipal garage. He had a strobe light with him. Unlike the last time he had been here, this time he figured he knew where to look.

Willie, who had been in the kiosk the evening Rivera died, was not there. Some other black guy was. In the spot where the Jaguar had been parked there was another car, a late-model red Chevy.

Benton identified himself to the other attendant and asked him to temporarily pull the Chevy out of the spot.

He did. Benton went immediately to the outlet and shone the light on it.

Nothing.

From a pocket he took a small screwdriver and unscrewed the screw holding the plate on. He removed the plate and shone the light inside.

There was a ganglion of red and black wires, but nothing else. If this was the source of the power, there was nothing left to indicate it, though some wires seemed less dusty than others.

Discouraged, Benton gave up.

An hour later, Benton was on his way to Huntington Hills. He had been able to contact DeVito's girlfriend, Linda, and she was going to meet him at the house.

She did. She let him inside.

He went over to one of the outlets above the medicine chest mirror. He unscrewed the plate and shone the light inside.

He expected to find just about what he had found at the garage: nothing.

But he was wrong. It was difficult to see, but because he was looking for it he found it: just inside the box, a slight scorch mark.

Jesus.

Benton calculated the possible path of a wire from the outlet to, say, a faucet.

It could be well hidden. Just connect it to the hot lead inside the outlet, then run it down the side of the medicine chest, then wrap it around a faucet.

It's electrically hot. All DeVito had to do was touch it. Bye-bye.

Benton turned. Linda was standing at the door.

"Did you find anything?" she asked.

"Yes," he said, "I believe I did."

On the way back to the city, Benton thought that bringing off something like this would require quite a bit of technical expertise. If he could find the man with that, he would find the murderer.

CHAPTER 49

Mary Muldoon was in the middle of watching *General Hospital* when the front doorbell chimed. She was annoyed. She had been watching *GH* for years now. The characters were like members of her family.

The front door was flanked by glass panels covered by curtains. She looked through one of the windows. She didn't recognize the person there. It was a pretty young woman with blond hair. There was a car parked out at the curb. There was somebody sitting behind the wheel. She assumed that the woman had come from the car.

She opened the door. "Yes?"

"Hello," the woman said. She was smiling. "My name is Meyers. I'm with the town. I hate to bother you, but we've had a report that there is an illegal apartment in this house and—"

"Bullshit!" Mrs. Muldoon barked. "Who told you this garbage?"

"I don't know who. We're just required to follow through and check."

"Now?"

"I'm afraid so."

"Bunch of baloney. I should call my lawyer."

"Look, Mrs. Muldoon. I'm just doing my job. I'm sure it's just spite work. I'll check into it and be gone."

Mollified somewhat, Mrs. Muldoon opened the door and let the woman in.

For the next few minutes, the woman followed Mrs. Muldoon from room to room, including a trip through the basement, to make sure that no part of her house had been converted to living quarters.

None had.

They were standing in the foyer.

"I'm very sorry," Ms. Meyers said, "to have troubled you. But we have to check these things out."

Mrs. Muldoon nodded. Most of the time she was showing the woman through the house there were those endless commercials on the TV. She had probably missed only a few minutes of the show.

"Have a nice day," Ms. Meyers said.

"You too," Mary Muldoon said.

She opened the door to let the woman out. For a moment she was puzzled, and then she recognized Jimmy Toolan and his wife, Veronica, standing at the door.

Mrs. Toolan was vaguely aware that the woman from the town had passed by them wordlessly. Then Mrs. Muldoon realized she wasn't from the town.

Mother of Jesus, she thought.

An hour later, Jimmy and Veronica Toolan were on Highway 80 heading east. They were happy. They had the number where her mother called Francie. Now they had to get the address. Just give it to a cop they knew and he could check it out in a reverse directory, where you could get an address from a phone number.

But the quicker they moved, the better.

CHAPTER 50

Based on the voice IDs she had gotten from the complainants, Barbara was able to get a court order to have telephone traps installed on each of the lines.

The trap worked simply: it was able to read the numbers of all incoming callers. Once Sergeant called, the contact at the phone company would call Barbara and she would get someone to get the search-and-arrest warrant for John Lock.

Barbara was a little concerned that the setup would upset the heart attack victim, Mrs. Archer, but once Barbara explained that they knew who the perp was, it didn't bother Mrs. Archer at all.

And she remembered him better than any of the other victims.

"I remember him at Monday novena. I don't know why, but I remember catching him looking at me. 'Catching' because when I caught his glance he quickly looked the other way."

"Do you have any idea why he's doing what he's doing?"

"No. It must have something to do with some fantasy or other."

Barbara thought that was very close to the truth.

Bledsoe was glad to hear that they knew who the perp was, that the phone traps were in place.

Barbara knew what Bledsoe's routine was. As soon as the collar was made he would call the media and give them the whole story, how teams of detectives helped capture a caller who was assaulting civilians for so many years, but it took the skills of Five Three detectives to finally run the perp to ground.

It bothered Barbara, but not that much. She had the respect of her peers, and of herself. That was really what it was all about.

After the traps were in place, Barbara made sure that she could be contacted twenty-four hours a day.

Then, the afternoon of the same day that all the traps were in place, she drove up to 242nd Street to see what the residence address of John Lock looked like.

She parked in front of another house fifty yards down the block where she could see without being seen.

The house where John Lock lived was an old house, just like the others on the block. It was Victorian style, with gingerbread trim, fronted by a small yard and a wrought-iron fence. It had a porch that led to glass doors with curtains on them. The house looked well maintained.

If you just looked at the house, it could have been thirty-six or thirty-seven years ago. Parked in the driveway was an ancient black Comet in very good condition.

Barbara stayed an hour, then left. No one had gone in or out of the house, though there was activity in and out of other houses on the block.

She drove back to the station house and went into her office.

Now all she could do was wait for Mr. Lock to reach out and touch the right someone.

CHAPTER 51

As he rode the elevator up in the Municipal Building, George Benton thought again that it had to be an inside job. Gold had a contact with somebody, somewhere, inside the City Development Corporation. Had to. Gold had to know about Parcel 19 from somewhere, and this had to be it.

Now he was about to take a flyer. A shot. Maybe it would pay off, maybe it wouldn't. But it was the first logical step.

This time, Benton didn't have to wait at all to see the director of the agency, John Vickers. He was ushered right in. He sat down in front of Vickers, and he laid out everything he had.

"Jesus Christ," Vickers said, agitated. "Goddamnit. Somebody from here is giving out inside information."

"You have no idea who Gold might be connected to in here?"

"None. As I said the last time you were here, Gold worked for us a long time before I arrived."

"Do you have any records of who he might have worked with when he was here?"

"Maybe," Vickers said, "but they'd be buried down in one of the warehouses on Johnson Street out in Brooklyn. This was before computers. You'd have a hell of a job to find the connection in that pile of paper."

Benton knew he didn't have a hell of a lot of time.

He thought: maybe he should just make a collar. But without any substantive proof Gold could get off. And Benton didn't feature having a guy like that on the street.

"Millie might know," Vickers said.

"Who?"

"Millie. She's been my secretary for years—and she was secretary to the director before me. She's been with the agency for thirty years. She might know who Gold knew back then."

Benton hesitated. "Is . . . is she discreet?"

"One hundred percent. Work for the city government for thirty years and you don't give out your name unless goaded."

"Okay. Let's call her in."

Vickers pressed his intercom. "Millie, could you come in here, please?"

A moment later there was a tap on the door.

"Come in," Vickers said.

The door opened and a woman Benton estimated to be about seventy—short, plump, and white-haired—came into the room.

She stood in front of Vickers' desk. Benton got the sense she was a little discomfited. It had occurred to him that she could be the leak from the agency, but he had to take a chance.

"This is Detective Benton," Vickers said. "He's looking into some things and thought maybe you could help."

"Yes, sir."

"Before we talk, though," Vickers said, "I must emphasize that what we say stays here."

"Yes, sir."

"Did you ever hear of David Gold?"

"David Gold? Sure. He worked here... fifteen years ago, for a couple of years, then he was a consultant."

"Did you know anyone who he knew at that time who's still here?" Benton asked. "Someone that he might still have contact with?"

"Sure," Millie said. "He knows Mr. McQuade."

"How do you know that?"

"Down through the years I know they've had contact. And I saw them together just the other day."

"Where?"

"Uptown, around 40th Street."

Benton turned to Vickers. "Who's McQuade?"

"Our assistant chief engineer. He's been with us twenty-five years."

"Would he know things?" Benton asked Vickers.

"Definitely."

"Okay," Benton said to Millie. "Thanks very much for your help."

"Yes, sir."

Millie left.

"Have you ever had any problems with him?" Benton asked.

"Yes—and no. He's always felt that he should have gotten the chief engineer slot, but he was always passed over and he groused about that."

"Why was he passed over?"

"His personality, basically. A very bright man, but he's an angry man—short-tempered. He's always on a soap box about race relations, but I think it goes lots deeper than that."

"What do you mean, race relations? McQuade..."

Vickers smiled. "Oh. William McQuade is black."

Benton was stunned, but, as usual, he showed nothing. *McQuade was black.*

"What, uh, color are his eyes?" Benton asked.

"Brown. Dark brown," Vickers said.

But, Benton thought, a couple of blue contact lenses could change that.

"What's his schedule for the next few days?"

"He goes into the field, but he'll be around, as far as I know, for the next few days."

"Thanks a lot," Benton said.

"Like I said, if it's him—please tell me first."

"No problem," Benton said.

He had one final question.

"Would McQuade know anything about electricity?"

"Sure," Vickers said. "He's an electrical engineer."

CHAPTER 52

Joe Lawless had just walked into the squad room when the phone rang. He picked up. It was for him. It was Arnold Gertz, calling from the safe house.

"Joe, you told me to call if there was anything out of the ordinary."

"Yes."

"Francie Collins can't reach her mother on the phone. Her mother hasn't called her, and she can't reach her. The phone keeps ringing, but no one picks up."

"She couldn't have gone out."

"Francie says all she does all day is watch TV."

"Good, Arnold," Lawless said. "What's the address?"

Gertz knew Lawless. He had it already. He gave it to him.

"Tell her I'll check it out. Meanwhile," Lawless said, "be very careful. Okay?"

"Yes, sir."

* * *

An hour later, Lawless was in an unmarked car—he didn't trust his own car to make it—approaching the street in Kings Park where Francie Collins's mother lived.

He pulled up a few houses down from the address given him by Arnold and walked up the sidewalk toward it.

As he did, he eyeballed the block. It was typically suburban, cars parked on both sides of the street, a few kids playing up the block.

There was a short overhang over the front door, and a single-step stoop. There were two newspapers on the lawn.

Lawless stood on the stoop a moment and listened.

He couldn't hear anything.

He felt the intensity starting to build.

Why hadn't the newspapers from two days been taken off the lawn?

He rang the bell. Predictably, no one answered.

The door had a standard nonsecurity lock. He could gain entry with a card.

But he tried the knob. It turned, and he pushed open the door.

"Mrs. Muldoon?" He called out.

No answer.

He entered the house, and as he did, just as a precaution, he pulled his 9 mm 16-shot Baretta. He took the safety off, then walked with the gun behind his right thigh. In case the woman was in the bathroom or something he didn't want to scare her to death.

He checked the living room, dining room, and another room, a bedroom on the first floor.

He called her name again, then went upstairs.

There were three rooms to check. One was empty, but the other two were bedrooms. The beds were made, unslept in.

He went back down to the first floor and flicked the light on at the top of the stairs to the basement. He went down.

He brought the Baretta out in front of him, though he seriously doubted anyone was there.

It was a typical basement. Tile floor. Oil burner. Electrical panel in one corner. Clean and neat, like the rest of the house.

Francie's mother was nowhere to be found.

Lawless walked slowly around the room, scanning to see if anything was amiss.

There didn't appear to be anything . . . but then he noticed something on the otherwise clean tile floor in front of the sink. He bent down and looked at the few drops.

They looked like blood.

He took a penlight out and looked at them more closely. Definitely looked like blood.

He stood up and shone the light in the big sink.

Nothing . . . except . . .

He spotted something caught in the drain. He reached in and picked it out. It was slimy.

He inhaled sharply. It was human flesh.

CHAPTER 53

Fifteen minutes after she had received the call from the NYNEX guy at the central office, Barbara Babalino and five other detectives pulled up in two cars in front of the home of John Lock.

As she had almost known for sure it would, the trap had caught Lock calling as Dr. Sergeant. He had called back Mrs. Archer.

Three of the detectives, one with a shotgun, went down the side of the house to the back. These old places had exits on the side and back.

Barbara and the other three detectives approached from the front. All carried handguns. In one hand Barbara had a search warrant.

She rang the bell.

No one answered.

Then, all to her right, she saw the curtain move in her peripheral vision.

"Open up. Police! Open up, or we'll take the door down."

The door opened, and standing there was a guy who looked like the prototype Mr. Milquetoast.

He was short, bald, and bespectacled. All he had on was a robe. He looked terrified.

"Mr. John Lock?"

He nodded.

"My name is Barbara Babalino. I'm a detective with the 53rd precinct. You're under arrest."

She read him his rights. While other cops cuffed him, Barbara entered the house.

It was like walking into a church, a dim, old church. Down a hall the walls were clustered with holy pictures of Christ, the Blessed Virgin, and all kinds of other saints.

The living room, through an arch to the right of the hall, looked more like a store where religious items were sold. There were maybe a hundred different religious statues, and more pictures.

All the other rooms were, to one degree or another, filled with religious statuary, articles, and paintings.

Upstairs, there were other rooms. One had its door closed, and Barbara could hear music coming faintly through it.

She opened up the door—and froze. It was amazing, like stepping into another time, a time before she was even born. For a moment she didn't know exactly what time it was—and then she did.

The Fifties. She knew it not only from what she saw, but also somehow, from her knowledge of all the victims who had been young in the fifties.

Barbara's eyes scanned the room.

She saw a couch and two chairs, the kind that are part wood and part upholstery. There was a floral pattern rug on the floor and, in one corner, a television—with a round screen.

On the walls were various deep-hued, emotionally dead paintings. One of the sea, another of a forest, another a farm scene.

184

There were old black and white photos on the walls, one of Harry Truman and another of "Joltin'" Joe DiMaggio standing at home plate, a picture Barbara remembered seeing many times before.

On one table was a brown radio with rounded edges. Lamps were made of driftwood. There was also a Tiffany lamp, the only one in the room that was on. It provided a dim light.

The phone, on a table next to an upholstered chair, was a heavy black rotary type.

Barbara looked at the number. It began with the letters of the alphabet, like numbers did in the Fifties.

There was one curtained window. It had a shade with a scalloped edging pulled down.

The only sound in the room was a female voice singing "Tennessee Waltz," which Barbara remembered from records advertised late at night on television. That's Patti Paige, Barbara thought.

This was, obviously, where Dr. Sergeant made his calls. His heart of darkness.

Barbara felt a surge of sadness. She realized something. The person who used this room had never really lived.

Why he did what he did was another question. There were a lot of questions.

CHAPTER 54

William McQuade was in his private office on the fifth floor of the Municipal Building. He was looking down at some cost estimates on a new housing project that was to be built in Manhattan. The estimates were obviously bloated, and, he also noted, the companies had fixed themselves with token darkies.

There was no question in McQuade's mind that these bidders were honky motherfuckers, but there was no way he could do anything about them. All he could do was pass them on to Vickers, and Vickers would make no motherfucking waves. The estimates would be approved, more overpriced housing would go up in New York, and no nigger boys would get rich working on the motherfucker.

Sometimes McQuade closed the door to his office. He got a charge out of making all those honky motherfuckers in the bullpen wonder what he was doing, like maybe calling his motherfucking securities analyst to see how his shares of AT&T were doing.

But today he had kept the door open and he became

aware that someone had stepped into the doorway. McQuade kept his eyes down. It was a little game he played. He liked to make the person uncomfortable, so he would feel like an intruder. Then when McQuade did look up he was in total control.

He looked up—and was surprised.

It was Vickers, and his eyes were angry.

"McQuade," he said, in a tone that confirmed he was pissed—and he usually called him Bill—"there are some people who want to meet you."

A tall good-looking guy dressed in spiffy clothes stepped into the doorway, then the office.

"This is George Benton," Vickers said, "a detective with the New York City Police Department."

Another guy stepped in. He was huge.

"And this is Detective Gertz."

McQuade was shook, but he hid his reaction. He glared at Benton, Gertz, and Vickers.

Then Herbert Kellner stepped into the doorway. McQuade felt the blood drain from his face.

Herbert Kellner looked at him. Kellner's face drained of all color, and for a moment he couldn't speak.

"My God," Kellner said. "My God! That's him! The witch doctor! Except for the eyes."

McQuade's eyes narrowed, his lips drew back over his teeth.

"What the fuck are you talking about?"

The statement was uttered with force and righteousness. But McQuade knew that it sounded hollow.

An hour later, McQuade was in a small room off the squad room at the Five Three. Benton—with Arnold Gertz observing the proceedings—questioned McQuade about his relationship with Gold.

At first, McQuade said nothing, but as time wore on he started to see something clearly: his ass was going to be in a bind. These fuckers had an eyewitness ID of him, and once they got into probing his relationship with Jew Boy—a name he privately used to describe Gold to himself—he was going to be up the creek.

McQuade came up with a solution.

Tentatively, using all his skills as an actor—something he had done on an amateur basis—he told how Gold had enticed him into doing the deal. He told how he had been vulnerable: he was a gambler and was into loan sharks. So he went along with the deal that Gold offered him.

The detective said nothing for a long time while McQuade laid it all out.

McQuade said he had known Gold for a long time. One day he mentioned to Gold that the Parcel 19 he owned was going to be very valuable. The city was going to buy it for a hospital complex.

Gold had thanked him and then made the suggestion: if McQuade helped him, Gold had a way to get most of the proceeds of the sale.

Kellner, Gold told him, had been in a mental institution once before—he had a nervous breakdown—and it would be fairly easy to scare him into dropping his interest in the property. That's the way the contract among the partners was structured.

If the other partners, Rivera and DeVito, would not scare so easily, they would have to be iced. Gold had a scheme by which McQuade would make believe he was some sort of witch doctor. Gold had devised a method whereby, if killing was necessary, it would look like the witch doctor killed them. Their deaths would be a wedge to make Kellner do what Gold wanted.

"Gold also figured," McQuade volunteered, "that he could take control of other properties he and Kellner were partners on. He could just ice Kellner, but then the deals were structured so that if he died his beneficiaries would get the property. He figured he could terrorize him out of those too. He wouldn't need to be killed."

Benton asked how DeVito and Rivera were killed.

McQuade confirmed the M.O. A thin wire carried an electric current and caused cardiac arrest.

"Whose idea was that?" Benton asked.

"Gold," McQuade said, "like everything else."

Benton was pissed, but he refrained from saying what he really wanted to because the interrogation was being transcribed.

It was one sentence:

"You're full of shit."

CHAPTER 55

Toolan figured the best time to go in was at night.

He had no idea how many cops were guarding the Collinses, but it didn't matter. Whacking one or two would make things just as hot as killing a dozen.

A very good crew would be required for the job. He had recruited four button men and three trusted Bronxies. There were two brothers, "Little Fish" and "Big Fish," Pavese, Joe "The Horn" Buscaglia, and Leo "The Lion" Maggio from the Alabanese crew. The three Bronxies were Ronnie Bittner, Walter "Crazy" Hartten and Andy Colen. All were heavy hitters and could take heat.

Toolan knew it was going to cost him a lot of bread. But it was worth it.

Everything had been cleared by Antony Bulletti, capo of the Alabanese family. They didn't want Collins doing a pigeon act in open court either. That could maybe expose a few loose threads. If the feds started to pull on them something might unravel.

Toolan and his crew arrived in the morning of the

planned hit. They had driven up in cars with New York plates, but Toolan was glad to see other cars with out of state plates. This was tourist country, and they wouldn't stand out like sore thumbs.

There weren't many cops around. They all seemed to be state troopers or the like—uniforms.

Toolan noted that their sidearms were .357 Magnums, one of the most powerful handguns in the world but no fucking good in a firefight.

In addition to revolvers and pistols, every single one of the crew carried Uzis—untraceable—with silencers. Any troopers trying to face this crew would be hopelessly outgunned, and Toolan thought it highly likely that the cops guarding Collins would be outgunned too.

Certainly they would be surprised.

Toolan drove by the address he had gotten from Mike McGrath, a cop he kept on a permanent pad. The house was on a typical street in Laconia, which, as far as Toolan could see, was mainly a bunch of one-storey buildings in the center of town.

The house, on a corner, was set back off the road, which was okay with Toolan.

There was one other house nearby. If possible, they would whack any witnesses in it.

Double okay was that the rear of the house had a yard and there were woods behind it. Toolan quickly decided that if he could approach through the woods, under cover of darkness, it would be ideal.

Once he decided this, he spent the next hour or so trying to see if there was a back way in.

There was, and it was perfect. The woods behind the house extended maybe two hundred yards. Toolan and his crew could approach the house through the woods.

There was no question in Toolan's mind that Jerry Collins was in the house. Toolan had seen three cars parked in the driveway, one with New Hampshire plates and two with New York plates.

Toolan considered what to do with the bodies. He thought that maybe he should Houdini them, but maybe not. What purpose would it serve?

Toolan also planned the escape route. The whole area was covered with snow, and it was cold, but it was not snowing now and the roads were clear and dry. Just a few minutes after leaving the house they would be out of the town, driving toward one of the superhighways that headed south.

Toolan and the crew were finished looking things over by mid-afternoon. They had rented a couple of motel rooms, and they just sat around, watching TV and eating.

Toolan was also thinking, thinking that word would filter back onto the street and it would increase his reputation beyond what he ever thought he could achieve when he was young. Very few people had the balls to pull off an operation like this.

It made him feel good just thinking about it.

CHAPTER 56

Barbara questioned John Lock in one of the interrogation rooms at the Five Three. Normally, one or more other detectives would have been present in the room. But Barbara had sensed that it was best to question Lock alone, the only "witness" a tape recorder.

She tried to be as sensitive as possible but still get the job done, because she sensed Lock felt terrorized. He worked his hands nervously, he was constantly biting on his lips, and his eyes flitted this way and that.

The overall goal of the interrogation was to get Lock to admit to certain things that would be relevant to the case against him.

But Barbara, who had majored in psychology when she was in college, and had once considered being a psychotherapist, was mostly interested in why a man would pick up a phone ten thousand times to make nasty, obscene calls? And why would he then change his pattern?

Barbara got nowhere the first hour or so. Lock seemed too scared to say anything.

Chinese food was brought in, and they ate. Then Barbara continued to question him.

Answers started to emerge.

"You live alone?"

"Since mother died."

"When was that?"

"Three months ago."

"I'm sorry," Barbara said.

"Thank you," Lock said. But there was no sorrow in his eyes.

"How long did you live with her?"

"All my life," Lock said flatly. There was something chilling in his voice.

"How old are you now?"

"Fifty-three."

"So," Barbara said, "you devoted your life to her."

"Yes," Lock said, and smiled. But it was not a happy smile. Beneath it Barbara sensed profound bitterness.

"Why did you make these calls, Mr. Lock?"

Lock looked at her. He was undecided, Barbara thought, on how to respond. Finally, he did.

"What calls?"

"Mr. Lock," Barbara said, "have you ever heard of mud sheets?"

"What are they?"

"They are records of local calls. We're going to subpoena them—and they go back years. We also have records of toll and long distance calls. We'll know about everyone you called."

Some of the color went out of Lock's face.

"It really will be better if you speak honestly. Or, you can stop right now and get an attorney."

Lock blinked rapidly.

He spoke. His voice was thin and low. "I don't know why. I would just be seized by it. Like I had no control over it."

Barbara nodded. "What did you feel?"

"Anger," he said.

Barbara nodded. She had the feeling that she would get nowhere if she tried to probe his sexual feelings. But linked to anger as they were, she could imagine what they were like.

She had an insight: an obscene telephone caller was just like a rapist—except there was no physical abuse of the victim. And, in a sense, sex had nothing to do with the rape. It was a power trip, an anger trip.

"What I don't understand," Barbara said, "is why you changed your pattern. When you first called, you didn't know the women, but over the last seven weeks, you knew them all."

Lock's eyes dropped to the floor. He seemed embarrassed. It was a long time before he spoke.

"I don't know. I just felt like it."

"Why these particular women?"

Lock smiled, and for a moment Barbara saw nothing in his eyes but sweetness and love, almost as if, for the moment, he had returned to that earlier time in his life.

Barbara felt something move inside her.

"I . . . remember," he said, "how they looked in their blue and gold uniforms . . . I . . ." His voice trailed off.

"What about the room, the one with the fifties stuff in it. Did you always have that?"

"No, I created that special to make the calls from."

"How long ago did you create it?"

"Two months."

Of course, Barbara thought. It was after his mother died. His pattern changed, and the room was created after his mother died.

"Were you angry with them?"

"I don't know. I used to think about what it was like to be with them . . . I liked them. When I was young I liked them."

The word came to Barbara: transference. That's what psychologists called it. People would transfer feelings they had for parents onto other people. If the feelings were good, fine, but if the feelings were bad . . .

Barbara thought she had the beginning of an understanding.

Lock wanted a relationship with women, but he must have been terrified by and angered by his mother. Maybe he *felt* that every woman was his mother, that to get involved with anyone was to get involved with her.

So he didn't. But all these years he had harbored hatred for his mother, which he transferred onto the women he called. She had an idea.

"What about now? When you started to call them? Did you still like them?"

"I thought I did, but they made me angry."

"Did you think you could have a relationship with one of them?"

Lock looked at her and smiled slightly, his face reddening. Barbara knew that she had as much of an answer as she would ever have.

There was nothing more to say.

"Mr. Lock, do you want to call an attorney? I'm sure he'll be able to arrange bail."

"Yes, I'd like that."

CHAPTER 57

At darkness, Toolan and his specially picked crew got into their two cars at the motel and left for the safe house.

It was completely dark by the time they reached the area.

They parked the cars on the far side of the woods, and then all seven men, led by Toolan, slipped into the woods.

The plan was for one of the button men, Little Fish, to ring the back doorbell.

Toolan and Big Fish would be beside him, out of sight.

Little Fish would ask for directions to Moultonboro, a town Toolan had seen the name of when he first came up.

As soon as the guard relaxed just a little as he talked to Little Fish, Toolan and Big Fish would step into the doorway and whack whoever was there. They would go inside, followed by the rest of the crew. The crew would know where at least some of the cops were from having looked in the back windows.

As they walked toward the house, Toolan couldn't help

but notice the moon and stars. He had never seen so many stars in his life, except when he was doing a bit in Greenhaven. Up there you could always see a lot of stars.

There was too much light, but he liked the way it reflected off the snow.

Toolan was feeling on edge, but good. He looked forward to personally whacking Jerry and Francie. He did not like the idea of whacking the kids, but that was necessary.

He generally enjoyed killing a lot, especially when someone deserved it, like now. Yes, he was going to enjoy clipping Jerry.

At the edge of the woods, Toolan could see the lights in the house. They would be in the open as they crossed the yard, but they would not be exposed for long.

Toolan hesitated. To the left, about twenty yards away was the adjacent house and a shed of some sort. The lights were out. It was impossible to tell if anyone was there.

Toolan looked to his left and right, and then he waved them on out of the woods toward the house.

They were five yards from the rear of the house when the sound boomed. A bullhorn. Someone was speaking on a bullhorn, and through the shock and fear Toolan felt he recognized the voice. Lawless. A single sentence.

"Put your guns or your brains on the snow."

The crew members momentarily froze, then were ready to fire, but it was impossible to tell where the voice was coming from—or where the guns were.

Toolan hesitated, then dropped his Uzi on the ground.

The others followed suit.

Then, powerful strobe lights came on in all the windows of the adjacent house, and uniformed cops, all with long guns, started to come out of the shed.

Then Lawless appeared, a shotgun on his hip.

Toolan wanted to kill him, but he knew that he was fucked.

"Even if you got to the house it wouldn't have done you any good, Jimmy," Lawless said. "There's no one there. Everybody was expecting your visit."

Toolan glared at him.

EPILOGUE

Almost a year after Lawless collared Toolan, the button men, and the Bronxies in New Hampshire, five major Bronxies, were convicted on 57 of 60 racketeering counts.

The sentencing of Toolan was laughable.

The judge, Chester Knabb, upbraided Mary Lee Baxter —who, in a very rare move for a federal prosecutor, spoke at the sentencing—for asking the judge to sentence Toolan to 150 years.

"I can't do that!" he said, "the law doesn't allow that!"

So he only sentenced him to three twenty- and one ten-year sentence to run consecutively. Toolan was thirty-eight. As one courtroom observer put it, "There is no way he will exit prison vertically."

Just before he left the courtroom, Toolan's eyes met with Joe Lawless's. Toolan tried to smile as if to say "fuck you," but it didn't work. They both knew that the real twinkle was in the eyes of Joe Lawless.

* * *

John Lock had no previous record, but there was no way that the judge—Burton Jones, a pretty tough one—was going to let him walk. Indeed, he could have done some heavy time. The District Attorney considered bringing an attempted murder charge against Lock for the heart attack Mrs. Archer suffered, but he decided that case wasn't winnable.

They were able to convict Lock on a variety of misdemeanor charges, and the judge sentenced him to six years, three of them suspended.

The judge got a big laugh when he suggested to Lock that he be careful about whom he called from the prison.

Lock was sentenced to serve his time at Riker's Island, but not among the general prison population, which would have made dog meat of him. He was segregated and made to serve time with a variety of high profile prisoners such as Bernhard Goetz, the subway gunman, and Joel Steinberg, the child killer.

The only person he called was his lawyer.

When Benton arrested Gold, he tried to oil his way out, but once he learned that McQuade had blamed him for everything, he started to point his finger at McQuade.

The name of the game was save your own ass.

When the dust had cleared, Benton more or less figured the following:

McQuade had told Gold about the potential value of Parcel 19.

Gold wanted it, and he entered in a partnership with McQuade. They probably worked out the scheme together, but the cardiac shock trick was undoubtedly McQuade's.

Both men were sentenced to life, and Benton thought they were lucky that New York State didn't have the death penalty. It had been a classic case of pre-meditated murder. And it had also been a real whodunnit, just what he had hoped for, a case he could sink his teeth into.

As it happened, it was to end up a pretty good year for

George Benton. Lawless had invited him over for a Christmas dinner, and he had accepted.

But he planned to spend Christmas Eve at home with Alien Nation, who would be making out really well this Christmas. Benton had bought her a variety of toys, some of which were impregnated with catnip. He liked to watch her go bananas.

As he walked down the block toward his apartment, though, he had felt depressed. A double homicide had come in—a grounder of the worst order.

Besides, Christmas was not the best season for Benton. It was great if you had memories, but they had to be the right kind.

He stopped at his mailbox.

There was something from Publishers Clearing House telling him he was the potential winner of millions of dollars.

Terrific, he thought. What greater gift?

And a card. He opened it.

On the front was a picture of cats dressed like Santa Claus. Inside it said:

Dear Daddy,
    MERRY CHRISTMAS AND HAPPY NEW YEAR
                            Love always,
                                Beth

Tears came to his eyes. Merry Christmas to you, honey, he thought, and love always.

About the Author

Tom Philbin is the son and grandson of cops. He lives on Long Island.